Halldór Laxness

A Parish Chronicle

translated from the Icelandic by Philip Roughton
with an introduction by Salvatore Scibona

archipelago books

Published by agreement with Licht & Burr Literary Agency, Denmark
on behalf of Forlagid, Iceland.
First published as *Innansveitarkronika*, 1970

First Archipelago Books Edition, 2026

Library of Congress Cataloging-in-Publication Data available upon request.
ISBN: 9781962770514

Archipelago Books, 232 3rd Street #A111, Brooklyn, NY 11215
www.archipelagobooks.org

Cover photograph: Walter H. Trevelyan
Typeset in Granjon

The authorized representative in the EU for product safety and compliance
is eucomply OÜ, Pärnu mnt 139b-14, 11317 Tallinn, Estonia,
hello@eucompliancepartner.com, +33 757690241

This work is made possible by the New York State Council on the Arts with the support of
the Office of the Governor and the New York State Legislature.

Funding for the publication of this book was provided by a grant from the Carl Lesnor
Family Foundation. This publication was made possible with support from
the Hawthornden Foundation, the Nimick Forbesway Foundation,
and the New York City Department of Cultural Affairs.

This book has been translated with financial support from

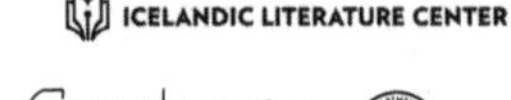

PRINTED IN CANADA

A Parish Chronicle

Introduction

Einginn fær mig ofan í jörð
áður en ég er dauður.
(No one puts me in the ground
before I'm dead.)
—Þorsteinn Erlingsson

In October 1969, Halldór Laxness was in Rome doing what came naturally to him whenever he could get to his favorite city: shopping for women's shoes. A clotheshorse even in his hard-up and ardently communist early days, he was at sixty-seven flush, and could now buy what he liked. But the state of European fashion depressed him. Nothing suited his taste. Certainly not the shoes, which he found "deliberately ugly."*

About the fate of his work he had lately been in outright despair. At twenty-nine he had promised in a letter, "I *shall* become a great writer in the eyes of the world or die!"† But

* Halldór Guðmundsson, *The Islander: A Biography of Halldór Laxness,* trans. Philip Roughton (London: MacLehose Press, 2008), 427.
† Ibid., 174.

in a recent essay he claimed never to have had any real success in his home country, where he believed he was "now rightly forgotten by those few friends who once hoped that I would achieve such a thing."* More than once he had sworn off writing novels for good.

If he hadn't had such grandiose ambition, would he have been so prone to grandiose disappointment? Or so immune to evidence that in the eyes of the world he had done fairly well? After all, he had won the Nobel Prize fourteen years before and was probably the most famous Icelander since Snorri Sturluson, the thirteenth-century historian and poet and one of the few medieval Icelandic writers whose names we know. By anyone else's estimation, Laxness's books had sold robustly in Iceland for years.

Nonetheless, it was true that the international readership Laxness had once craved hadn't quite come to him. In the United States, for example, nearly all his dozens of books were out of print or had never been translated. The ego that had made it possible for him to write and publish his first novel at seventeen was the same undying tormentor that made it excruciating to accept anything from the world short of continuous acclaim.

By the time he arrived in Rome that October, fresh off a publicity junket in Denmark, he had lived about twenty years

* Ibid., 426.

longer than his father had. He might reasonably have assumed he was nearing the end of his productive life. He didn't know that he still had six more books to go, or that the many readers he had once hoped for would begin to find his work, especially in the English-speaking world, only after he would die twenty-eight years later in an Icelandic nursing home in 1998.

Since then, the new American edition of his masterpiece *Independent People* has gone into forty-four printings. Through reissues and new translations by Philip Roughton of major novels including *Iceland's Bell* (2003), *Wayward Heroes* (2016), and *Salka Valka* (2022), the big, ambitious, often political or historical, but always wickedly funny novels of Laxness's mid-career have become available to English-language readers. For us, it's as though this man has been publishing new work for ninety years, since *Salka Valka* was first translated from its Danish version and published in London in 1936.

The shoes were for his wife and daughters back home in Iceland. (He often stocked their wardrobes when he traveled.) His shopping companion was Fru Dinesen, an intrepid spirit right out of the sagas, who had left the Danish farm where she was raised; gone to England to work as a housekeeper; moved to Italy; married an Italian who couldn't support her; been widowed at forty-four; and by a bewildering mixture of nerve and luck (and despite the interference of two world wars) gone on to make herself a prominent Italian hotel proprietor, all while raising six children and publishing four memoirs.* Five years earlier, the king of Denmark had knighted her. Laxness had been visiting her hotels in Rome since the thirties. She was ninety-seven years old.

One wonders if Laxness considered at least her a success, or any of the dozens of brilliantly drawn Icelanders in his novels who are born with nothing and die with less but in the meantime live with the self-possession and spiritual vision of saga heroes or saints.

In any case, the other thing that came naturally to Laxness in Rome was to write a novel, which he could do there in sun-drenched rooms with the windows open. He evidently could not help but write there. His biographer, Halldór Guðmundsson, states that Rome always worked on him like a drug. The torture of his egoism about writing seems to have made the act of writing all the more necessary; it freed him from himself. When a novel got going, Laxness once wrote his second wife, it "lives in me like a separate world."†

The world that came alive in him that October was *A Parish Chronicle*, a short novel he had drafted six years before and

* Gejl, Ib: *Marie Dinesen* i *Dansk Kvindebiografisk Leksikon* på lex.dk.
† Guðmundsson, *The Islander*, 373.

set aside. It begins around the tenth century and sprints like a racehorse with light-footed gusto into what was the present day, all while maintaining the canny facade that it is nothing more than a vignette of sleepy parochial history, a sketch on the back of a brochure. Perhaps inspired by Dinesen's age and resilience or by the ancient city around him, it's imbued throughout with admiration for what is very old, spiked everywhere with skeptical humor that somehow doesn't diminish that admiration.

Even in the nineteenth century, when Iceland was the poorest country in Europe, everyone there could read. The relationship between Icelanders and their literature and language can seem to foreigners a little insane. "This may seem strange," one Icelander told an American television reporter in the 1980s, "but the Icelandic language is the very reason why we are staying here."* Contrary to Laxness's doomy feelings about his impact on his countrymen, the week he died, an appreciation of his work in the country's leading newspaper concluded, "The day Icelanders forget the writing genius of Halldór Kiljan Laxness, they will no longer fulfill their role as a nation."†

Icelanders speak one of the world's oldest languages in continuous use and elect representatives to a parliament that has

* NBC News, *Today Show,* aired 1986.

† "Sá sem lifir ekki í skáldskap lifir ekki af hér á jörðinni," ["He who does not live in fiction will not survive here on Earth], *Morgunblaðið*, February 10, 1998, 33.

a claim to being the world's oldest surviving legislative body. But geologically the country could hardly be younger, being entirely volcanic. Don't bother looking for fossils; almost no sedimentary rock has had time to form. The sagas of Icelanders—plotty, laconic, often heart-rending—constitute one of the oldest literatures in any language still commonly spoken. Laxness was the heir not only to the language and setting of the sagas but to their humanity, their outrageous understatement and charm. Nonetheless, reading his novels even decades after his death, they land on the mind with the shock of the new. Readers who think they know the limits of Laxnessian style or what he seemed to believe will keep being surprised.

Throughout his career Laxness changed his mind about nearly everything that mattered to him. Politics, religion, love, prose style. He seemed to thrive on the meat of his own sacred cows. While he was working on *A Parish Chronicle*, he wrote to a Swedish scholar, "I have had a little novel in the works since the autumn, driven on by the same need for renewal that has always plagued me."*

A Parish Chronicle would be published in the original Icelandic in 1970. It is presented here in English for the first time. It represents yet another radical shift, in narrative perspective and ideals, for a man who never came close to writing the same

* Guðmundsson, *The Islander,* 441.

book twice. It is his only novel in which he himself appears,* all but invisibly, like a sprite.

Crammed with humor and pathos, it tells the story of a church bell as much as of a parish and a nation. Centuries ago in Mosfellsdalur Valley, near the farm called Laxnes (where the writer born Halldór Guðjónsson grew up and from which he later took his name), a little church is ordered demolished by the Danish crown in order to consolidate the parish with another nearby. More than a century passes before the authorities arrange to carry out the decree. But a few of the locals will have none of it.

Their cunning, and their persistence in holding onto what remains of their patrimony after the church is leveled, may go a little way toward explaining to foreigners how Icelanders have managed to survive in such a treeless, wind-scoured, famine-prone place for more than a millennium, or how they have maintained a language mostly unchanged since the time of the Viking raiders who first settled there.

The reader may wonder how much of this book is true, in the most secular and least inspired sense of the word. In fact many of the characters—even Big Gunna, one of the great larger-than-life paupers of Laxness's oeuvre—did live in Mosfellsdalur and went by the names Laxness gives them in the book.† Nevertheless, the first Icelandic edition included the prefatory note, "References to

* Ibid., 443.

† Innansveitarkrónika "Sögupersónur," https://innansveitarkronika.is/sogupersonur.

named individuals writings documents places times and events do not serve a historical purpose in this text." He plainly didn't let the historical record impede invention.

Laxness was a writer and a person of unembarrassed self-contradictions, a patriot given to blistering criticism of his countrymen; a doting father who in his twenties got a farm servant pregnant and seldom had anything to do with the daughter who came of it; a loyal friend who published a fawning defense of the Soviet state even after he had watched the secret police abduct one of his comrades from her Moscow apartment in the dead of night and take away her infant daughter during the Great Terror. We know this because he wrote about it, after he changed his mind about Stalin too.

If Laxness often wrote about what was wicked, ugly, even horrifying, he did so out of a habit of finding beauty in little else. As he said of one of his protagonists, his "cause was evil from almost every point of view except his heroism."* The challenge that some readers confront when starting his bigger books—on which *A Parish Chronicle* may work for future English-language readers as an urgent inducement to get moving—is sometimes whether they want to endure so much hardship and cruelty on nearly every page. But his heart never leaves these people, and

* "Sá sem lifir ekki í skáldskap," 33.

the experience of reading him is of a singular, wry, unstinting sympathy, especially for characters at their most blockheaded or deranged.

This contrast opens the territory for the kind of humor and pity he is so good at. “I don’t think a person needs to be eating all the time . . . It’s a bad habit,” says Gunna, who has just nearly died of exposure and has not eaten in three days.

A Parish Chronicle is a late vein of Laxnessism, as free of his previous ideological entanglements as he could make it. Around the time it was published, when a television interviewer asked if he had betrayed his youthful ideals, he answered, “I hope so.” Here, he’s as humane as ever, as interested in human folly, but now much less interested in correcting it. It is the work of a writer with nothing to prove, only to tell. It looks from the outside like a modest book. It turns out to be a major book in the grandness of its modesty.

Salvatore Scibona
New York City, 2025

1

Egill Skallagrímsson's Head

After Iceland's national hero and chief poet Egill Skallagrímsson had been resting comfortably in his grave mound for some time near what is now the main road through Mosfellsdalur Valley, in an area called Tjaldanes because travelers camp there, Christianity came to the country.[1] At that place, two rivers converge and run as one between high banks out of the valley. The poet's bones were then exhumed and brought from the mound to a church, even though he had been a heathen.

A church had originally been built at the foot of Mosfell Peak at the place later called Hrísbrú, where it stood until a landslide fell onto the homefield there in the 12th century. After that, it was moved to a hill a bit farther to the east, now part of the Mosfell churchstead. Hrísbrú itself was a croft of Mosfell, on Mosfellstún west of the landslide.

When the church was moved, so written sources say, human bones were found under the altarplace of the old Hrísbrú Church; they were much larger than other people's bones, and the residents of Mosfellsdalur moved them to Mosfell along with the church. Elderly folk believed them to be the bones of Egill Skallagrímsson.

An anecdote in the medieval *Egill's Saga* testifies to the robustness of those bones: the priest who was in charge of their above-mentioned exhumation in the 12th century, Skafti Þórarinsson, picked up the skull and placed it on the churchyard wall; the skull was extraordinarily large. Yet what was even more surprising was its great weight; it was ridged all over like a scallop shell. Wanting to test the skull's thickness, Skafti took a heavy hand-ax and struck the skull as hard as he could with its hammer end, trying to break it, but the skull only turned white where he hit it, and neither dented nor cracked, says the saga verbatim. Egill's bones were buried at the edge of the churchyard at Mosfell, and no one has seen them since; foresighted people have said that they will only be found again on Iðavöllur.[2]

If you look at Mosfell now, you would think that the church had been there on the hill, its steeple silhouetted against the clouds, since ancient times. This, however, is not the case. Again and again this church disappeared from the hill. Over and over, it was thoroughly erased from the pages of history and omitted from the laws of God and man, failed to appear in written documents, was neglected in oral tradition. If any church has ever been able to cry out, justifiably, "My God, why have you forsaken me?" it is Mosfell Church.

When a church was rebuilt at Mosfell in these our own times, only around eighty years had passed since the last church disappeared from the hill; perhaps someone who had been baptized in the old church in 1888 was still living, although no one came forward to say so. The first time the church disappeared from the hill, two hundred and fifty years passed before the good word was heard there again. In the 13th century, the church still stood unchanged in its place, says *Egill's Saga*, but more than a hundred years later, it is no longer mentioned in church inventories. In the *Vilkin Inventory*, from the latter part of the 14th century, this church no longer exists. Not very long afterward, Mosfell ceased to belong to the church, but the farm is listed in a register of the landed property of a rich lady in the west, Ólöf Björnsdóttir.

When a church was built there again during Lutheran times in the 16th century, everyone had forgotten which saint originally owed it, and of course, the saints had been abolished by then. And not only had the saints disappeared, but also the Holy Cross itself. Our Lady is lost and gone, along with Egill Skallagrímsson's head, and there is no one to answer to but the Danish king and Luther.

Here, the story will be told of how the church was dismantled and razed to the ground for the third time in the latter part of the 19th century. It will be shown how powerful exponents worked together to destroy this church ever since the Danish king ordered its removal in 1774, although one hundred and twenty years passed before that order was implemented. For almost four generations, consequential parties laid their hands to that plow, such as the government in Denmark, the Icelandic Alþingi time and again, the church authorities one after another, bishops and deans as well as lesser parish authorities; finally, local farmers and honest housewives and robust men belonging to this parish, until no one remained to defend this church but a certain aged farmer at Hrísbrú named Ólafur Magnússon, and an indigent girl, a maid of the priest at Mosfell, named Guðrún Jónsdóttir. Then, it must be said, that poor church fell. Still, many believe that God's wisdom and long-suffering achieved a certain victory in this matter here in Mosfellsdalur, even if it took some time, and the world might well take notice of this, although there may in fact be something to the viewpoints of those who think differently.

2

Ugly Land, Evolution Unknown

The hill at the southern foot of Mosfell Peak upon which the church stands hoards more sunshine than other hills. Even at winter solstice, there is often a spot of sunshine on it. The so-called "Partfarms," on the other side of the valley opposite Mosfell, are shadowed by the peaks at whose northern feet they stand.

Those who live at the southern foot of a mountain are usually quite perky, while those who don't see the sun for ten to eighteen weeks a year can be pissy, as the locals might say. In such a shadow lay the three Partfarms, where, in our day, a sanatorium was built for orphan children and overburdened mothers. Although it was on the dim side at the Partfarms, where the poorest people in the valley always lived, they were located in a geothermal area, and the heat from the Partfarms hot springs is now measured in figures reminiscent of the calculation of light years in outer space. In the past, people here in the valley lacked most things now considered essential to human life, except for a hundred thousand million tons of boiling-hot water. For a hundred thousand years this water, more valuable than all coal mines, ran in torrents out to sea. Mosfell Church had rights to this tremendous source of heat, and the madam at Mosfell had bread baked there in the hot sand. A worn old shovel standing there in the sand century upon century was used to bury the dough quickly and then retrieve it as fully baked bread. In still weather, steam ascended from the hot springs and lay like creeping fog over Kirkjumór, which was the name of the marshy, flat floor of the valley (now called Víðir).

From Mosfell Hill, one could have witnessed the lights of Reykjavík growing in number from when a few wretches in the service of the Danish monopoly sat there by their train-oil lamps in the 18th century, until now, when the capital of Iceland gleams by its bay with greater luster per person than in other capitals. That splendid city is now heated with the hot-spring water of the Partfarms crofters and has more bathwater per individual than any other city in the world with the exception of the capital of Kamchatka.

East of Mosfellsdalur Valley begins the wilderness, where the church owns heathlands, rocky deserts, and mountains adjoining the country's desolate uplands. Heading straight east from Mosfell, not a farm is seen until Seyðisfjörður, on Iceland's east coast.

Undoubtedly, butter and honey used to drip from every blade of grass for the spirits in this valley, as in Iceland's other valleys before people came to this country. Grain was grown here for hundreds of years. In the 14th century, the farmer at Laxnes, in the middle of the valley floor, was obliged to provide two barrels of ale to the governor at Bessastaðir and transport it to Þingvellir for him to drink at the Alþingi. Following centuries of overexploitation of the valley's crops and vegetation, with nothing grown to replace them, ale-making came to an end at Laxnes in the 15th century, and the land continued to be overused into modern times, when the homefield was used as a greensward from which turf was cut and sold to Reykjavík.

At the end of the Middle Ages, after the land had been gnawed down to its roots and defaced by every available means of destruction, as is currently being done in Vietnam, and soil erosion left entire districts barren, people began living again like Robinson Crusoe. They contented themselves with rowing out to sea and hauling in "those damned four" instead of growing grain and brewing ale. And thus did they plod through the centuries, even forgetting to bathe for seven hundred years, despite having more hot water than any other nation on earth.

In such a valley, there was in fact no way forward and no way back. The theory of evolution had not yet been born and the goal was to stand still, at most to resemble one's grandfathers.

The priest at Mosfell was the de facto head of the valley, whether people liked him or not, in some respects outside of human society, and on the authorities' payroll. The Icelanders had instinctually looked up to booklearning ever since ancient times, when they were rich and wrote books, and even if the national morale was now hostile to booklearning and services were no longer being held in Latin at Mosfell Church, most people had somehow learned to read. These days, Latin, despite the priest being said to know it, was like magic that has lost its power. Ideals hadn't been invented yet; such a word didn't exist. There was no such thing as "the beauty of nature" either; no one would have understood the term even if it had existed, which in fact it didn't. Those were the ages when people believed that Búland Peak was ugly and that an abominable place like Lake Mývatn had been created because the devil pissed toward the sun, while ghosts were sent to Gullfoss. It never occurred to anyone in Mosfellsdalur to lead others in anything, be it good or bad. No one born and raised in this valley held a seat on the district council until Andrés at Hrísbrú, as far as those now living can recall. The farmhouses were built of turf, although one or two had a cold guest room where guests were made to sit until they were chilled to the bone. Everywhere, people slept in the family room, often on blocks of stacked turf. One might say that those people were content with their simple clothes and the taste of their plain food; and even if they heard cocks crowing and dogs barking in other districts, they didn't long to go there, as it says in *The Book of Tao*.

The capital was referred to as "down south" and to go there was to "go south," although it's located in a roughly westerly direction from this district. For a short time, the main road lay on the northern side of the valley, leading to Borgarfjörður and then northward. Pack trains took that route in the spring and autumn, some from distant counties where people have large farms and money and go south and buy horseloads of goods in cash at favorable prices. Those pack trains always had an otherworldly air to them.

And pack trains from distant districts continue to trudge through the valley. Sometimes the people of Mosfellsdalur sat on their doorstones in the summer, fixing ropes and doffing their hats to long-distance travelers. Jónas Hallgrímsson once rode by, and afterward composed this poem:

The farmer having ropes to fix
sits outside and knots does tie.
His wife with hay piled up in ricks
from travelers would some kerchiefs buy.

Of course, most women in Mosfellsdalur will have had one silk kerchief—in fact, the woman in the village whom I least expected to have a silk kerchief did indeed have one; she will be mentioned later. Old locals say that it wasn't unheard of in this place for a farmer who had cut a horseload of hay to take it south and sell it for schnapps. In the evening he would set off home from the south, splayed over his packsaddle, flask aloft. Sometimes it rained; he would fall off his horse into the Kortúlstaðá River, or at least often woke the next morning in a green hollow there at the ford in the river. Upon waking, his throat would be a bit dry and his flask empty, his horse lost and sometimes his dog, too. He would take a drink from Kortúlstaðá and set off on foot up the valley for home, and when he arrived at his farmyard, his horse and dog and wife would be there to greet him. But not until my day did anyone ever go so far as to sell the sward from his homefield. As for a kerchief for the wife, no one has ever said anything.

3

Not Even a Poor Little Angel; Traffic Begins

Now we come to a man named Ólafur, whose patronymic was Magnússon, born in the Gullhreppur district. He lived at Hrísbrú. It was mentioned before that there was nothing but scree between the Mosfell and Hrísbrú homefields. At Hrísbrú, one can hear the ringing of the Mosfell church bell, as well as the barking of the priest's dog and the crowing of his cock, better than at other farms, and Farmer Ólafur never tarried in getting to Mosfell when the bell was rung. When he went to church, he always wore his Sunday best: a short, rather wide jacket of homespun cloth with homemade bone buttons, collarless and buttoned to the neck, and regency trousers like Napoleon the Great. He had narrow mutton chops, as would have been fashionable for men just after the turn of the previous century. He didn't speak well of people in general but was considered peaceable himself, apart from always being at odds with the Mosfell priests over the encroachment of their livestock and other injustices he felt they inflicted on him—and that they felt he inflicted on them. He outlived many a priest, and although they were all different from one another, he never made any distinction between them, instead speaking about each of them as if he were a group, and always with the same title, in the plural: "those devils." Ólafur of Hrísbrú never fenced his homefield, but was all the more ready with a dog and cog rattle, especially when it came to the priest's livestock. If Ólafur spotted movement in the scree off the main road, he would think it was the priest driving his sheep onto his land and launch a counterattack. He would sic his dogs on unfamiliar sheep that slipped onto the Hrísbrú homefield, which they seemed to be adept at doing, and on occasion, they chased the whole flock up the mountain, where not a single blade of grass grew, and drove them into a huddle there. Horses bolted at the clicking of the rattle and hurtled over everything in their path, while cows sometimes ran into quagmires at the noise. Reverend Stephensen once gave Farmer Ólafur a talking-to and from the pulpit urged folk to show good neighborliness and fence their fields, because "good fences make good neighbors." When parishioners went to the priest at the rood screen after mass and thanked him for his sermon, Ólafur of Hrísbrú said: "You devils have no problem letting your horses chew my fields bare, but since when have you ever managed to show anyone a single, poor little angel here on your homefield?"

It had been many years since the road from the south through Tungumelar and the Hrísbrú morass was closed. At one time, that road led behind the buildings at Mosfell, over Hestbrekkur up to the farm Skeggjastaðir, where it turned down along the homefield wall north over the Leirvogur River. Sometimes people spent the night at the farm Þverárkot by the road below Svínaskarð Pass, then set course for the pass the next morning and from there crossed through Kjós to Borgarfjörður, as the route lies northward.

At Hrísbrú, seven adjoining turf buildings turned their gables toward the farmyard, but only the entrance's gable was made entirely of wood; this was called the "farmhouse door." Fronting the row of buildings was a pavestone walkway, quite narrow, in fact, but whoever stood on it was safe.

Few people passed by Hrísbrú without seeing one or more of its residents standing outside the buildings. Farmer Ólafur himself often stood by the open storehouse door, sometimes knitting a sock or whittling logwood into rake teeth with his jackknife, and putting the shavings in his pocket or else eating them.

"Who's there?" he asked without looking up if he heard someone squelching through the mud that reached up to the walkway.

"Some lads," answered passersby, according to national custom. Many, however, stopped in the mire and started chatting with the man. His sons would join the group, bearded and indistinguishable from their contemporaries Karl Marx and Bakunin. The household also included a father-in-law, what with it having daughters, too, although they were invisible. The father-in-law was a distinguished doctor from Suðurnes, and he sometimes told about the wondrous sheep-dung treatments and peat-treatments that they prescribed there in the southwest, and how these remedies came especially in handy when university-educated doctors, medical students and midwives had given up. This father-in-law, however, was the cleanest of all men and resembled the famous Danish priest and poet Grundtvig, with a clean-shaven face framed by a white beard that grew from his chin and jowls to his chest and venerable white hair down to his shoulders. I mention famous men with faces typical of the period so that the reader can look them up in their *World History* and see what kind of face I mean.

The folk at Hrísbrú were rather pleasant of manner apart from old Ólafur when he was wrangling with the priest, but showed no particular interest in dragging people out of the mud bordering the walkway and inviting them inside. They asked for news of sheep from all over the country, because life in Iceland was, as it still is today, all about sheep. For example, when talking about the weather, it was only from the perspective of how it suited the sheep. Good weather was the weather that was good for sheep. A good year was one in which enough grass grew for the sheep. A beautiful landscape in Iceland is one in which there's good pasturage for sheep. People's livelihoods and outlooks on life were determined by that creature. The Hrísbrú folk were kept informed by travelers of the circumstances of sheep all over the country, and for their part, told stories about the welfare of sheep in the Mosfell district. They remembered exactly what the weather had been like for the sheep year by year for thirty years back. Those people never wore coats, but their woolen cardigans and sweaters stood up to water and wind like the fleece of an Icelandic sheep. All homemade and in the sheeps' natural colors, mainly russet.

Long-distance travelers considered the Hrísbrú morass one of the greatest obstacles on the route northward. The original farmhouse had undoubtedly been built on marshland in days of old, but the marsh had never been drained, perhaps because a sacred spirit had inhabited it from the beginning. After people settled there a thousand years ago, the waterlogged ground in front of the walkway became intermixed with various of the substances that are a byproduct of humans and livestock. A dung heap that had been created in antiquity in front of the cowshed door at the east end of the row of buildings continued to mingle its liquid materials with the rest of the farmyard mud, with no clear distinction between them. Now the old turf farmhouse has been forgotten and replaced by modern houses for humans and animals, along with a refrigerator, milking machine, and bathtub;

motorized vehicles are parked on a gravel-covered parking lot in front of the farmhouse door. No one hears anything about the old morass anymore; no beard is seen in the farmyard.

No one, folk thought, was as skillful at taking hay from the stackgarth as Bogi at Hrísbrú. In the winter, he spent a large part of the day smoothing out the straws in the hay wall. He rounded out all the corners, leaving no hard edge anywhere. He often took hay from a stack starting at the bottom and working his way upward, so that moisture didn't form on the earthen floor, and as winter wore on, the hay under his hands took the shape of a bowl on an uneven base, and finally resembled a footed shot glass; the stack's load-bearing capacity, however, was never diminished. Bogi was frequently found running his hand over the surface of the stacks, like a man stroking his jaws to check if he has shaved well enough. Many people came to the stackgarth to admire this work of art.

This Bogi was cheerful toward everyone and never harassed man or beast as far as is known. He saw rather poorly; folk said that he had "working vision" but not "reading vision." Often, he couldn't tell people apart, and spoke the same to everyone; he had an especially hard time distinguishing between teenagers. Yet no matter whom he talked to, he never ventured into topics he knew nothing about.

Andrés was considered the spokesman for the father and sons at Hrísbrú and answered for them with the greatest assertiveness, both there in the farmyard and elsewhere. As mentioned earlier, he became the first native of Mosfellsdalur to hold a seat on its district council. He even owned books, and was given more books when he turned sixty. He often brought out the work *People and Culture* by Páll Eggert Ólason, which he received as a birthday present from the district, and let people weigh the book in their hands to feel how heavy it was. Many people envied him his seat on the district council. He bought himself a full-length overcoat to wear to the council meetings. Yet after sitting on the council for several years, he said: "The district council is no entertainment committee, especially now that both traffic and competition are making themselves felt in the district."

4

The Soul and the Sickbed

It has been claimed that at this farm on the main road, where it wasn't the custom to invite people in, but instead where bearded heroes stood guard on the pavestones and left those who showed up to fend for themselves, there was in fact a single soul behind most things. It was the wife of Ólafur of Hrísbrú. No one knew her, passersby had never seen her, and some concluded that such a woman didn't exist. However, many of the area's residents had seen her in previous years when she still walked around her house, quiet of speech but with a firm grip on everything, yet in some way a guest in her own home, being from the north; the national poet at Bæsá who translated Milton and Klopstock was apparently her grandmother's brother.[3] How was it that she came from the north and married Ólafur of Hrísbrú? Nothing has ever been said about that. A person or two remembered far enough back to have seen this woman sweeping the smooth, hard-packed dirt floors at Hrísbrú with a swan's wing before Christmas. Perhaps the slough outside the front door, whose depth no one knew, along with the mud bordering the walkway had become too much for her. One day after all of her children had reached adolescence, she lay down in her bed and didn't get up again; the sickbed has been one of the most important social institutions in Iceland since the country was settled. It was said that the woman had been bedfast for eighteen years. Folk also said that at the head of her bed, she kept a sock containing the household's cash, and in a narrow but fairly tall box she stored the pound of sugar that every farm must have. Her children, the bearded men, were said to speak to her in hushed tones. Her name was Finnbjörg, and in censuses and old documents it is often written as Fimmbjörg. Her husband supposedly addressed her as such, and one boy who had moved to the area thought her name was "5 Crags."[4] Her bed was in the section of the family room nearest the gable, where the window was. Old Ólafur lived with his sons in the middle section, whose door led to a long, dark earthen passageway. He talked to her from his bed, and was now starting to sound a bit hoarse. Although Ólafur was considered "farmyard cold," he was said not to be "family-room cold." He could frequently be heard speaking to the woman from the farmhouse's front door, whence his voice would carry through the earthen passageway, or else from out in the farmyard, his voice slipping in through the window. Sometimes he did so from up on the roof, while patching up the turf or smearing it with cow manure or spying on those devils the Mosfell priests, who always seemed to him to be driving their sheep onto his land. No one knows for sure if the woman ever heard her husband, because a reply never came.

5

Difficulty Unknown

It was rare to meet the Hrísbrú men when they weren't in the middle of farmwork, either going to the sheep sheds or coming from them with moss in their beards, filling the hay crates, fixing ropes at the storehouse door, maybe banging something together. But their hands were never so tied that they didn't have time to natter with a traveler from Kjós about how it went for him bringing back his sheep from the mountains, or to ask a person from Borgarfjörður about the weather up there last year and the year before that and the year before that; or a northerner how the weather was there in the north during the Great Spring of Feebleness twenty years ago, when the sheep here in the south died from torpidity. The ups and downs of the country's sheep were discussed as one might normally discuss the circumstances of better-placed people in society: unctuously and ceremoniously, but perhaps not always with deep feeling. Sakes alive, how smoky it is on Seltjarnarnes now! I say! Maybe they're doing some rendering, or boiling dogfish. Maybe their oil has caught fire. What's that rancid stench coming from the Mosfell priests now? Hardly hung lumpfish, for great men like them; you don't suppose they got their hands on a whale, those devils?

They never walked straight and never bent-backed, but there was no denying that they stooped slightly at the knees. Their dogs were generally harmless and lay on the pavestones outside the front door with piss-bored expressions, watching passersby. It was only when Farmer Ólafur sicced them on the priest's sheep that they transformed, like the swine spoken of in Holy Scripture. These men spent an inordinately long time going and looking after their sheep, even taking into account their rather laggardly gaits. While herding, they might sit down on a mossy tussock in the middle of Mosfell Heath and start tearing into a rock-hard cod's head, which is one of the most complicated challenges in Iceland, so much so that now only five people in the country are thought capable of it, and so time-consuming that whoever does it is hungry again by the time he stands up from the table.

It's a wonder that men so unadept at walking should spend their lives competing in a long-distance race with swiftly bounding sheep. But incredible as it may seem, those stiff-legged men, only moderately sharp-sighted and prone to congestion, always had it better in the race against those lightning-fast creatures, which was, I think, because they always moved so slowly that the sheep lost interest in the game; partly also because although the sheep is stubborn, these men were a sight stubborner. They never lost patience even if one of those creatures ran away from them up a scree-covered mountainside, mad with fright. They never talked about it being difficult; for them, the concept "difficult" didn't exist. It might be added that wise authors consider it a superstition sprung from incapacity that there are such things as difficult tasks; tasks are difficult only if they're done by the wrong methods. Although they couldn't see well, no sheep ever escaped them on the mountain; instead, they all returned to the valley without showing any signs of fatigue or feeling out of breath. They were incapable of hurrying, or of being late.

Now that the haymaking had begun, the men of Hrísbrú could be seen in their homefield at the time of day when no one else was up and about apart from one or two milkmen, who set off shortly after midnight on their journeys south with a wagonload of milk cans. It was never clear to me whether they'd just gotten up, or hadn't gone to bed. The Hrísbrú men hardly moved, or so it looked, no doubt because the field was so tussocky, unsuitable for those used to swinging away at the grass with their scythes. It was strange to see those bearded men toiling there at three o'clock in the morning, almost motionless in the grass, hunched over their scythes, perhaps asleep. The outcome, though, was that that tussock patch was left close-mown and the Hrísbrú household never lacked hay. I still remember them sharpening their scythes out in the field shortly after midnight. For that job, the scythe's cutting edge had to be thinned in order to hone it better; the edge was flattened with a blacksmith's hammer on an anvil. The anvil was thrust into a tussock, which the hammerer sat astride. The hammering rang out like a rather high-pitched bell, carrying well even to distant places in the still of the night. The peal of metal striking metal was most welcome to the newly woken thrushes, which rooted for earthworms in the scythe tracks of those men while the grass was still damp. This is the music you remember when you live to be a hundred.

6

The Authorities Waken

Now it should be told that many years had passed since the king issued an order that Mosfell Church be done away with. Back then, the people of Iceland were instructed to consolidate churches throughout the country for reasons of economy. Now, there happened to be, and had been for a long time, two churches in the Mosfell district, each at its own end: the one in Mosfellsdalur up under the heath, the other at Gufunes in the Sund area, by the sea. In the central part of the district, there had been no church since Catholic times, when the chapels at Suður-Reykir and Varmá were discontinued. Kjalarnes to the east of Kleifar belonged to the Mosfell parish, while the deanery was called Kjalarnesþing in accordance with the old division of districts. For a long time, the country's church administration, as well as the deans of Kjalarnesþing, had hemmed and hawed over mergers and other relocations of churches in these parts, despite such measures being thought beneficial for the country's coffers. It appeared as if people chose their salvation over these coffers, reacting with indifference and evasiveness to the Danish king's ingenious ideas concerning church building as they did to various of his other ingenuities, even if it often ended with the king prevailing. Now, over the course of the last three hundred years, people had reconciled themselves to the faith that the Danish king had proclaimed here, and which had resulted in the king making the Icelandic bishop his footpage while the deans became errand boys of the government, albeit of varying faithfulness. Yet despite Lutheranism having been unqualified to answer the question as to which saint Mosfell Church was dedicated, or to reveal to people even so much as one poor little angel, and however great the misery of the priests became in both life and soul, these farmers could not brook the fact that a distant, foreign king was tampering with churches here in Iceland, and it was said that the people of Mosfellsdalur would stand shoulder to shoulder in ensuring that God was kept in the place where he belonged, which was in Mosfell Church, where the head of Egill Skallagrímsson rests.

In the hundred-plus years since the order came from Denmark that Mosfell Church was to be demolished, the Icelandic population had sometimes been rather spiritless, and the country's government, for its part, didn't have the vigor to gather up all the small churchsteads the Danes wanted dissolved, but let it suffice to do away with the churchstead of Skálholt, which was then called the capital of the country, as well as Hólar in Hjaltadalur in the north. Piddling churches dotting the country's hills, such as the one at Mosfell, would have to wait. In addition, during those hundred years, various other concerns demanded attention: the Haze Hardships, Napoleon the Great, Jörundur the Dog-Days King, courant currency and sheep scab. But by the end of the 19th century, the population had begun perking up so noticeably that the royal decree of 1774 was put back on the agenda, this time in the Alþingi, and it turned out that although this decree had admittedly not been implemented, it had never been repealed. So it happened that on May 12, 1882, the Alþingi in Reykjavík decided that in order to lighten the load on the national coffers once more, the merger of the two churches in Kjalarnesþing, Gufunes and Mosfell, must now be seriously pursued, provided that two-thirds of the congregations consented to it. At a church meeting of Kjalarnesþing held at the Seminary in Reykjavík on January 11, 1884, participating representatives, deans, priests, and leading parishioners resolved that action should now be taken in the church affairs of the people of Mosfellsdalur. No one opposed the resolution.

Reverend Jóhann Þorkelsson was then priest at Mosfell. He claimed not to have noticed any negative reactions on the part of his parishioners toward the church merger, yet added that farmers in Iceland were hesitant by nature, and it wasn't always easy to hear what they muttered, much less get anything substantial out of them. Their thoughts on the matter would presumably be clarified at a meeting at which the required vote would take place.

Following the district assembly of the church authorities, a meeting was held here in Mosfellsdalur, at which the farmers of the Mosfell parish were to vote on the issue. But in this royal dream that had lasted since 1774, serious complications were constantly arising. Due, however, to constant pressure from the Kjalarnesþing dean, the Þórarinn who wrote *The Book of Þórarinn*, fifteen of the twenty-five farmer-parishioners of Mosfell Church were successfully gathered into the sitting room of that church's parsonage in 1886.

That famous dean, who had enlightened the people of this country with his book, now used all his erudition and eloquence to impress upon those farmers the necessity recognized by the church leadership and national government of the merger of the churches, and lamented the lassitude that had prevailed in this district for over a hundred years when it came to accepting the gracious wishes of the authorities in this matter. Some took snuff, others blew their noses or spat, and a few scratched themselves. But no one let a word slip from them on this issue.

Then a vote was taken. First, a proposal was put to the vote to the effect that anyone who did not express his will for or against should be considered as agreeing to the merger of the churches in the Mosfell district. On this proposal, three or four people voted, none against. In the vote that followed, on the issue itself, six people voted in favor, while three were against. Six were silent. It was a lackadaisical turnout, hardly fulfilling the Alþingi's requirement of a majority in order for the merger of the churches to become legally binding. The meeting was dissolved on the grounds that attendance was insufficient and the will of those few who did attend was ambiguous. The dean declared that there was now no other option but to gather the votes of the parishioners in writing, without further meetings. Reverend Jóhann at Mosfell, along with the chairman of the parish council of Mosfell Church—Farmer Kolbeinn of Kollafjörður—were tasked with collecting parishioners' signatures regarding the unification of the churches in the Mosfell district and urging them to express their opinion for or against the demolition of Mosfell Church.

7

The Start of the Church War

As mentioned earlier, these events took place shortly after the start of haymaking, when the nights are bright. The weather was benevolent, with beautiful dry spells, but the grass was rather too dry during the day and zealous haymakers were up at the crack of dawn to mow their fields while they were still wet with dew.

Early one morning at this time, as the sun was rising between three and six o'clock, there is a loud knock on the door of the parsonage at Mosfell. The priest and his household were sound asleep.

In a sleepy haze, Reverend Jóhann calls out "God be with you, who's there?" according to national custom.

"Some lads," came the answer from the farmyard, according to the same national custom. "Now it's time to get out of bed and answer for yourself."

According to excerpts from a letter that Reverend Jóhann wrote to his dean, Reverend Þórarinn at Garðar, which were printed in a newspaper long afterward, this visit went as follows:

In the farmyard stands Farmer Ólafur Magnússon of Hrísbrú with his scythe perched on his shoulder, the tip of its blade pointing straight up. There is still grass on the blade, meaning that the mower has come straight from his field. He sticks the end of the snath into the ground in much the same way you might imagine Gunnar of Hlíðarendi doing with his halberd when he wasn't swinging it.[5] A little farther out in the farmyard, near the lychgate, stands his son Bogi, who was acting as his father's squire on this expedition. Bogi is holding a rake with bits of hay in its teeth, having been following his father through the field and raking the newly mown hay when both received a higher calling. When Reverend Jóhann comes to his door, Farmer Ólafur opens his mouth there in the farmyard and addresses the priest as follows:

"Is it true that you're going to demolish Mosfell Church, Jóhann, you devil?"

"I don't think that's entirely correct, my dear Ólafur," replies Reverend Jóhann, "but it is true that the king and the Alþingi have ordered the unification of this community's churches, and that this is supported by the governor, the bishop, and all the deans, and in fact by most sensible farmers in the district."

"Isn't this Egill Skallagrímsson's church, and wasn't Egill's head stolen from us at Hrísbrú originally?" asks Farmer Ólafur.

Reverend Jóhann replies that unfortunately, we no longer know which saint Mosfell Church was dedicated to originally.

Ólafur says: "Even if Egill Skallagrímsson isn't a big enough saint for you Mosfell devils, he's good enough for us at Hrísbrú. And even if you've stolen the church from us, we consider ourselves to own so great a share in it that we will never allow it to be torn down. We have come here from our homefield at Hrísbrú because we cannot bear to live any longer under such oppression. Tell those devils that. Here, there shall be a fight. Blood shall meet blood."

Reverend Jóhann then replies: "It is good and beautiful to fight for a good cause, my dear Ólafur, especially if we have turned to the Heavenly Father and asked him to lend us true understanding and the right weapons."

"I've already gone to a blacksmith," said Ólafur of Hrísbrú, "but those rascals are so degenerate that they no longer know how to forge swords."

"And who do you suppose is going to fight with swords now, my dear Ólafur?" asks Reverend Jóhann.

Ólafur answers: "I'm prepared to do so, as is Bogi."

"Well, indeed, my dear Ólafur," says Reverend Jóhann. "It crosses my mind—perhaps I should wake Gunna, although it's still early, and ask her to put on some coffee."

Then Ólafur says: "Do you and those other devils think that my relative Egill Skallagrímsson went and drank coffee when he was in a fighting mood?"

"Unfortunately, I have no ale, as Egill used to drink," says Reverend Jóhann. "But good coffee is good if it's good."

Then Reverend Jóhann asks his visitors to wait a bit and disappears into the house. Moments later, the priest's teenage maid, named Guðrún Jónsdóttir, comes to the door rather scantily clad and asks if the guests wouldn't like to drag their asses into the kitchen with her for some washed-knickers water.[6]

This Guðrún Jónsdóttir, illegitimate but said to be of the Stephensen family, was then around twenty years old and was considered a unique person in her community both at a young age and ever afterward. Now a few words shall be said about this girl, just for the time being. She was very comely—"fair as the fells" as folk have taken to saying nowadays—had a difficult childhood, but early on started toiling away for her bread and butter and her handiness drew praise, especially when it came to cutting peat. She was a heavyset woman and had the physical strength of vigorous men. She went from farm to farm and took jobs that others weren't eager to do, and had such a pleasant personality that everyone wanted her near; yet despite her use of coarse language, no one ever took offense at the things she said. More about her manner of speaking in due course. Guðrún Jónsdóttir lived and worked her whole long life in this district, without ever taking any pay for her labor, as far as anyone knew, and all her life, she had only two sets of clothes: an everyday one and another for church, like the Jesuits. She knitted herself socks and shawls from the wool of a few ewes that belonged to her, and for outerwear, wore a fustian jacket and tied a shawl over her head; her church skirt was made of homespun, dyed black, while her cardigan was of fine cloth, although I don't recall having seen the woman wearing a kerchief round her neck, which was otherwise obligatory with such cardigans. Every now and then a farmer would give her a lamb, and she would personally make hay for them and house them on farms where she had connections. Eventually, she acquired a chestnut mare. She was in fact a capitalist because she was never formally employed at any particular farm, but instead worked on her own terms, free of obligation to whomever hired her—what in those days was called a "freewoman." That title had an air of distinction, even if it may have been imaginary. In any case, she certainly was independent. More about this woman soon.

"What are you doing milling about with your poky little snaths on other people's doorsteps in the middle of the night, you wretches?" Guðrún Jónsdóttir recalled having said to them when she was asked about this visit much later.

The visitors had sat down in the kitchen and were waiting for the coffee.

"We're thinking of getting you a husband," old Ólafur then says.

"Oh, what poltroon might that be, you old scoundrel?" Guðrún Jónsdóttir remembered asking. "What sort of a man do you suppose would go and marry such a fussock as Big Gunna?"

"Well, someone like little Bogi over there," says Ólafur.

"Oh, you shouldn't need to bring a scythe with you for that, don't you think?" says Gunna.

"All I have is a rake," says Bogi. "And my father's scythe wasn't aimed at you, Gunna."

"Thanks for pointing that out, my poor little man. Let me refill your cup," says Gunna.

Ólafur: "There's nothing for it but to keep those devils in check. For me that's what has always proved best against those Mosfell priests. You can't get bloody anywhere with them unless they're scared."

"I could tell they were quite happy to be given coffee, those poor mutts," said Guðrún Jónsdóttir many years later when she was asked about these events. "They slurped up a few bowls of that slosh of mine and snuffled and snorted once or twice. But they didn't thank me for it afterward, or give their regards to the household. They said they had to keep mowing the field while the grass was still damp, those sorry sheeplings." Guðrún Jónsdóttir showed them to the door. She asked: "You haven't forgotten anything, you poor things?"

They didn't answer.

After finishing their coffee, they found the scythe still standing there in the farmyard as they'd left it. Ólafur pulled it out of the ground and perched it on his shoulder, but this time with the blade's tip down.

Then they turned homeward, Ólafur leading with his scythe, Bogi following with his rake; they disappeared behind the farmhouse hill into the gully.

8

A Theological Excursion

That same morning, around the usual time that people in the district started to stir, Reverend Jóhann rode out to collect signatures in support of the unification of the churches. He and the parish council chairman, Kolbeinn of Kollafjörður, had arranged to meet. Reverend Jóhann spoke slowly and in a somewhat dusky tone, like a voice from the deep, whereas Kolbeinn of Kollafjörður had humorous anecdotes at his fingertips that got others laughing, all except Reverend Jóhann. Now, as is often the case when such worthies feel out their fellows, they encounter little by way of rebuttal from the other parishioners, and in fact, find most of them agreeable to the business at hand.

Presenting his case to the farmers, Reverend Jóhann said that he was tired of his tenancy on Crown land like Mosfell, with its related obligations and the other inconveniences that living on the authorities' bread entails; he informed them that he had now secured the purchase of Lágafell, where a church was to be built in accordance with the will of the king, the Alþingi, the governor, and the bishop, and hopefully also the Lord himself, as well as sensible people in this community. Reverend Jóhann said that he wouldn't levy a higher land tax than two krónur and would guarantee burial plots for the entire community in a new churchyard there for four krónur. The farmers asked if that rent was to be valid forever, and Reverend Jóhann replied that this lease was based on a rate set by the bishop and approved in Copenhagen. Many said that they would rather be buried at Mosfell for free. Reverend Jóhann said that God would be no farther away from his congregation at Lágafell, where there were unlimited resting places, than at Mosfell, which had only one small hill. Up until now, the Mosfell-district farmers had themselves been responsible for the upkeep of the churches at Mosfell and Gufunes, and in addition, had to pay two krónur per year for the church plot at Mosfell, which was absurd, and four krónur per year for the sexton; a total of six krónur per year at Mosfell as opposed to six krónur for time and eternity at Lágafell.

"You might say that once you've come to Lágafell, being in Heaven will be cheap," Reverend Jóhann concluded.

One farmer then asked: "Is it absolutely certain that we'll go to God when it's over here?"

Reverend Jóhann said that it was.

They went on to ask: "And why do we go to God? Have we earned it? And what business do we have there, deary?"

“We came from there originally,” said Reverend Jóhann. “It’s our home.”

In support of this idea, Kolbeinn of Kollafjörður told of a woman who took her husband Jón up to Heaven in a sack. Peter said that he didn’t want Jón there and was about to slam the door on the woman. But the woman stuck her foot between the jamb and the door and, by giving the sack a vigorous kick with her other foot, sent it flying through the doorway far into Heaven. Peter was stuck with the old fellow.

The farmer at Leirvogstunga then says, “So am I to understand, chum, that that woman had three legs? The one she stood on, another that she stuck between the doorpost and the door, and a third that she used to kick the sack into Heaven?”

Question: “Do those who go to Hell also have to pay six krónur?”

“We know so little,” said Reverend Jóhann. “In fact, we only know one thing. We belong to God and our home is with Him. But it’s open both ways.”

Then it was asked: “Can’t you priests pretty much spot in advance which people are going to Hell? If those of us who go to Heaven have to pay six krónur to buy a burial place for all eternity for those who go the other way, it’s a scam, even if a small one.”

“Few of us priests are so gifted that we can see with certainty who is fittingly fat and who not, to say nothing of seeing what is more," Reverend Jóhann says. "It's important to be fittingly fat, and not too gaunt, either. The rest we entrust to the omniscient God."

This was interpreted to mean that the gaunt ones would take the lower road because they tended to vilify God and men due to hunger, while the fat ones would take the same route, having gotten that way by sucking dry the houses of widows and orphans. But it could also mean the exact opposite.

Kolbeinn of Kollafjörður then tells the following story: "Once upon a time, a father and son were teasing horsehair. Then the boy says out of the blue: 'Is it true, Papa, that the Redeemer descended into Hell?' 'I don't know,' says the man. 'The priests have been saying that, anyway. We won't be letting that bother us any. We'll just keep plucking apart this horsehair here.'"

The result of this hunt for signatures, which brimmed with theological entertainment all day long and well into the evening, was, of course, what with two such estimable men having had a hand in it, that everyone signed their names to what they had either been reluctant to accept or voted against just a few days ago. A man or two signed with the proviso that the merger of the churches would hopefully not happen until a few years from then, when those who were now living were dead, and said that they put their names down in the firm hope that that would soon be the case. But everyone now knew both that their church stood on shaky legs before the will of God and man and that neither words nor oaths had any power against the fate determined for said church. It did soften the harshness of fate's sentence to listen to the persuasions of good men regarding this matter and not to have to yield before a show of force; it was, however, less certain whether anyone there lent his name to paper having been moved to do so by reason.

Kolbeinn of Kollafjörður told in a letter of his return home that evening, after he and Reverend Jóhann had said goodbye to each other following the day's achievements: "In the evening I rode over the Scree, past Hrísbrú," he writes. "The Hrísbrú men were standing on their walkway, repairing tools. 'Well, I say, you'd better sign your name now, Ólafur. Everyone else is already on paper.'

"Ólafur says: 'I've never signed, don't sign, and never will sign. My head is lying at Mosfell; it's the head of Egill Skallagrímsson that the Mosfell priests stole. That head shall never be broken.'"

"And what do you think, Bogi, will you be signing?" asks Parish Council Chairman Kolbeinn.

Bogi answers: "I will be leading my father's horse should he need to visit any other farms."

9

News from the Front. Mustering of Troops

"Well, what do you know! You two, father and son, making the rounds, weak-sighted as you are!" folk said to Ólafur of Hrísbrú the day that he came riding through the district with his son Bogi leading the way.

Never before had anyone heard of Farmer Ólafur of Hrísbrú becoming publicly involved in community affairs; neither had he sought a seat on any committee, nor had others sought for him to hold one. Like all Icelanders, he could read, but opinions are divided as to whether he could write; in the one document bearing his signature, there is no mention of it having been written by proxy. Some have claimed that now, when he rode through the district for the first time to muster the other farmers, he brought with him some sort of written declaration opposing the unification of the churches. There has been no confirmation of this and no document to that effect has been found archived. On the other hand, he spoke at length to the farmers and exhorted each and every one who had a serviceable cutting implement, even if only a spade or a shovel, a crowbar or pickaxe, to shake whatever dirt and rust they could off it and start sharpening it. Their dull, rusty weapons, though, might not be enough, he said, and therefore, he thought it advisable that people polish their old pieces if they owned any, or else, if they had the courage in them, to buy new guns. It was also very important that the women stand behind their men and have mugs of boiling urine at hand for burning those devils who ordered the destruction of Mosfell Church.

He also believed that people who didn't have the strength to keep an old parish church on their home ground going, and fight for it until the end, deserved to be torn to pieces by dogs and ravens. Those were the ones who sold their hay for schnapps, and next time they would sell the soil from their homefields for more schnapps—a prediction that seems to have come true in the Mosfell district in recent years. "Have people become so miserable," asked Ólafur of Hrísbrú, "that they can't bother their own sorry asses to hold on to a church in their own community, and in a famous place at that, where the head of Egill Skallagrímsson rests? Are these people more likely to maintain churches on deserted crofts down the valley where not even a dog would lie? What sort of kings and bishops and deans are they who exhort this country's rabble to tear down the churches of their fathers? And who are they that heed those devils who order such a thing? Soulless drunkards and horse tormentors, I expect, who from the very start have straitened the circumstances of widows and orphans here in this district. Into the light with them! Is the time coming when you'll never again be able to look a real man in the face in this backwater? Do you think those devils at Mosfell give a rat's ass whether you take the road to Hell? After all, they've now bought Lágafell and supposedly have papers from knackered old bishops and mingy kings in the previous century obliging you to work for free on building your own enemy church at Lágafell. To add insult to injury, they're going to cheat you out of six krónur by promising that you'll repose for all eternity at Lágafell. At such a place! As far as I know, it's been free at Mosfell until now."

When Ólafur of Hrísbrú finished speaking, he was grim-faced and gritting his teeth, looking like the mask that Henrik Ibsen put on for photographers in his later years, while fire burned in his red, purblind eyes; then he stepped behind a wall to relieve himself and spent no small amount of time doing so.

It has been argued that Icelanders are swayed little by rational arguments, and hardly economic ones, either, yet even less by religious rationale, but solve their problems by splitting hairs and arguing over irrelevant trifles, and become terrified and dumbstruck when it comes to the heart of the matter. On the other hand, they take on herculean tasks to oblige their friends and relatives, and were it not so, Iceland's rural communities would have collapsed many centuries ago. Yet there is one other type of reasoning that Icelanders willingly submit to as a last resort, and that is humor, even of the most imbecilic sort. At a ludicrous cock-and-bull story, Icelanders soften and start beaming; the soil of their souls grows fertile. For these reasons, the members of Mosfell parish were eager to consent by word and oath one day to a matter that was as remote from them as possible: because that friend of theirs whom they esteemed above God, Reverend Jóhann, asked them to do so. The next day, Ólafur of Hrísbrú appears straight from the ancient sagas and coaxes the community to his side with reasoning that was no less authentically Icelandic.

However one understands the revolution of the spirit that Farmer Ólafur's expedition brought about in the district, it is fairly certain that reason played no part in it, much less faith, and least of all were vested interests involved. Suddenly, people were uncertain as to whether it was right to demolish Mosfell Church, and at the same time, feared that by signing Reverend Jóhann's document, they had relinquished their head, which was the head of Egill Skallagrímsson, the head that Egill himself had ransomed. Unplanned meetings took place in undisclosed places seemingly by chance, at which, neither minutes were recorded nor speeches made; no one exhorted anyone to anything, and in fact, no account was ever given of this conspiracy, nor will that be done here. But everyone felt that something started stirring in the nation's soul from the day that old Ólafur made his rounds.

Concerning the Hrísbrú men, it may be said that although they lived beside a traveled road and heard news from many different places, they could in fact be taken entirely by surprise. Now it so happens that Kolbeinn Eyólfsson of Kollafjörður, parish council chairman, rides into the farmyard at Hrísbrú and greets the father and his sons. After the usual exchange of news, Farmer Kolbeinn takes out a new document that he had on him and entreats the father and sons to put their names to it. The first person on this document, as on the previous one, is he himself, Parish Council Chairman Kolbeinn Eyólfsson, and following his name, one could see those of all the householders in the Mosfell parish with the exception of Reverend Jóhann.

Unlike the previous document, this new one was not addressed to the bishop, but to the governor of Iceland. In fact, this second document requests the annulment of the one newly sent to the bishop regarding the church affairs in Mosfell. Yet it is worded as such: that hasty measures regarding this church be refrained from for the time being, including, hopefully, that the demolition of the oft-mentioned church not take place, or at least that its unification with other churches, for which plans are already in place and that the parishioners have been made to feel obliged to support, with their unpaid labor, no less, be postponed.

Those who send the governor this letter call it a rash act on their part when they, a few days ago, put their names to another letter, that time to the bishop, which had happened more out of untimely acquiescence to the parish priest than a careful consideration of arguments and reasoning. A public meeting held according to the stipulations of the legislature had shown that people were indifferent to innovations in church matters, and a legitimate majority in favor of those innovations had not been obtained at that legally convened meeting. Various people doubted that signatures gathered on documents could replace a resolution on this matter approved at such a meeting, as was prescribed in a law issued by the Alþingi; even if men signed their names to a worthless piece of paper borne to their homes, it would seem that such a thing had no legal force. The farmers request that they hereby be allowed to revise their position in a new document to be tendered to the governor of Iceland, in the hope that he, according to their submissive petition, would intervene in this matter as the nation's representative to His Highness the King.

10

Appraisal of the Church. Petition

An appraisal of the church that has been somewhat under discussion here was carried out by order of the dean at Garðar on the same days now told of, during the lamb-weaning in June, 1887. The appraisal record is signed by Parish Council Chairman Kolbeinn Eyólfsson and two others, and can be found among the papers of the Kjalarnes deanery from that time. Farmer Kolbeinn had his hands full that summer dealing with various issues related to said church.

The appraisal record describes the church as being 11 ells and 11 inches in length from gable to gable, making it 7 meters in modern reckoning. The width measures 9 cubits and 12 inches from wall to wall.

The exterior is considered more or less ruined due to rot, the groundsills are all rotten, the interior paneling unrotten apart from that closest to the entrance.

Ornamenta: altar (lock missing); pulpit; altar rail; pedestal for a baptismal font; altarpiece depicting the Redeemer's resurrection; worn chasuble, of velvet; one surplice; altar cloth of little value; altar cloth border, old and unusable; silver chalice with gilt interior, along with an old paten of the same; corporal, old; 2 candelabra with two arms each, of copper; glass chandelier, defective; two memorial plaques; a hymn board and number-storage box; brass baptismal font, dented; spade, tolerable; bell, undamaged.

According to the church's ledger, its funds amount to almost 2000 rixdollars, having been increased in recent years by land taxes, while nothing was spent on church maintenance.

Now this summer passes without anything of importance occurring in the affairs of the church just described. Until a rumor arises in the south that things are growing mucky in Mosfellsdalur. Nor is it mere gossip—old Gróa of Leiti's delight—rather, it has been firmly asserted that two letters signed by all the parish farmers there in the valley have been presented in the highest places, one to the bishop, the other to the governor.[7] These letters are said to be unique and extraordinary, for although they are signed by the same people and deal with the same subject, each asserts a different opinion on every point, as if in them, two stalwart opponents were met on the battlefield. Comparing the documents, it becomes clear that every man born of woman in Mosfellsdalur holds two opposing views on this matter and is prepared to fight for both of these causes, one on one day and the other the next, with a conviction and rigor that cannot tolerate compromise. Truth be told, whoever goes to the trouble of scrutinizing the letters and documents relating to this matter, in the archives of Kjalarnesþing and the episcopate on the one hand and the governor of Iceland on the other, will hardly be able to avoid rubbing his eyes once or twice.

The people of Mosfellsdalur's second letter, to the governor, is not officially sent to the bishop for comment until December 15 that winter. In the governor's remarks, in which he summarizes the main content of that letter, he references the Mosfellsdalur residents' idea that he, the governor, is the representative of the Icelandic people vis-à-vis the king and the church authorities, and that is why the people are now pinning their hopes on him when all else is failing. In his report to the bishop, the governor states that for his part, he believes it to be without a doubt that the entire parish is behind the petition, which concerns all the parishioners equally. The governor suggests that although these people were previously subject to other attempts at persuasion in this matter, and for that reason subscribed to opposing views for a time, every person in this country is free to change his opinion, each squarely in his own way, as well as many in common if they so desire and according to what their reason dictates to them, after having carefully considered the facts with regard to latterly available evidence. Likewise, if someone appeals to his Christian conscience, it must be respected, especially if it can be credibly demonstrated that such a conscience exists. Since problems have arisen with respect to the method of solving congregations' issues behind the backs of the congregation members themselves or against their will, then we suggest, says the governor, that we do not plunge straightaway into a solution to this matter. Secondly, it seems absurd to the governor that farmers in the Mosfell parish are urged to contribute their labor, uncompensated, to build a new church outside their old parish boundaries. It is always imprudent, in any matter, to introduce side issues that could conveniently be used by the opposing party to cast doubt on the matter's core. The governor suggests that compulsory labor for the construction of a new church could be interpreted by the farmers as an attempt to humiliate them. It would also be inadvisable to speak aloud about confiscating funds from Mosfell Church's modest holdings to hand over to the proposed Lágafell church, which, admittedly, did not yet exist. Better to keep this money in the custody of the episcopate for the time being. Finally, the governor reiterates the opinion that this matter may well be postponed until time revealed a more suitable solution.

It is not clear from the archives of the two offices whether the bishop replied to the governor's letter concerning Mosfell Church. However, after the governor sent the episcopate a copy of the Mosfellsdalur residents' second letter, the bishop does briefly mention it in one place in his letter to the dean of Kjalarnesþing, which still exists; he calls it "the petition of the residents of Mosfellsdalur to the governor." This was during the final years of the episcopate of Bishop Pétur Pétursson, who was then one of the wealthiest men in the country and such a great writer of sermons that he may be considered one of the few Icelanders who fully understood God. In a letter to the dean of Kjalarnesþing, Reverend Pétur Pétursson states that the Mosfellsdalur residents' letter to the governor expresses only "blind obstinacy." The bishop does not mention that all the farmers of the old Mosfell parish signed the document. The "leader of this resistance" is the bishop's designation for Parish Council Chairman Kolbeinn Eyólfsson of Kollafjörður, who, despite signing his name to the governor's letter a few days earlier, had, in another letter to the bishop, expressed a contradictory opinion. Ólafur of Hrísbrú is not mentioned at all in this context; perhaps he was not deemed worthy of having his name put to paper in higher places.

In the autumn, the foundation of Lágafell Church was quietly and silently dug, as well as that of the expected parsonage at Lágafell. In early spring, carpenters came from the south and erected the framework for the new church.

11

The Story of the Precious Bread

On June 29 of the same spring that Mosfell Church was torn down, the following article appeared under the heading "A Story of Precious Bread" in the weekly newspaper *This Century*, and anyone who feels like going to the library and reading old newspaper articles can find it there:

It so happened in Mosfellsdalur on a spring evening several days ago that a twenty-year-old girl by the name of Guðrún Jónsdóttir, a maid of the priest at Mosfell, who in fact resigned from his office after the church was demolished, was sent to collect pot bread that had been baking slowly in the warm sand of a hot spring owned by Mosfell Church south of the river, where the priest's bread was customarily baked. In a wooden bucket that she brought with her, the girl had another unbaked loaf of rye bread to exchange with the loaf in the sand, it being usual that when a fully baked loaf was fetched, another unbaked loaf was buried in the sand in its place. The bread was dark brown, and ordinarily weighed six pounds.

Now it should be noted that there was a dense fog, despite it otherwise being a bright spring evening. When the girl had exchanged loaves and was on her way home with the baked bread in the wooden bucket, taking the same route to the parsonage as she had hundreds of times before, she loses her bearings, and instead of continuing straight north as usual, she heads straight south and winds up in a marshy pass between two mountains, a place she doesn't recognize. She tries following streams but moves continually upward, until finally coming to wide, desolate heathland, uninhabited by men. These wild stretches of land, which belong to Mosfell Church and are used as summer pasturage by numerous rural communities, are commonly and collectively referred to as Mosfell Heath.

For quite some time, the girl thinks that she is on her way home to the parsonage and half-recognizes landmarks that she feels confirms it. When she finally realizes, however, that she has come twice to the same rock, the same stream bend or the same tussock, she starts becoming concerned. To make a long story short, the girl wanders all night over the heath, far from any human habitation.

Around that time the old church at Mosfell was being demolished, continues the weekly *This Century*. Carpenters had arrived for that purpose early in the day and there was a great deal of activity; the priest's wife had left and the priest was preparing his departure, as well, and perhaps few people noticed that there was a lack of bread. When it was discovered that a girl was missing, too, no one suspected that she was up in the mountains. At first it was thought that she was visiting relatives in the valley. Upon investigation, however, it turned out that this was not the case, and since the fog up in the mountains hadn't cleared, it seemed evident that the girl had lost her way. On the third day, the community sent search parties to find the girl. On the morning of the fourth day, her footprints were discovered on a bare patch of earth far up in the wilderness, and toward noon she herself was found sleeping on a heather-grown hill near the so-called Hengill Mountains. Some say that on bare ground not far away, she had written her initials with her finger in the dirt, G. J., along with a bit of a will.

By that time, the fog was slowly starting to thin. Two farmers, neighbors of the girl, came upon her as she lay sleeping with her bread bucket beside her and her hand clutching its handle. These farmers now roused the girl from her sleep, yet upon finally waking her, she didn't recognize the men and instead sprang up with panicked screams and took off running as fast as she could, bread bucket in hand. So confused was she still that she not only thought she'd never before set eyes on those old acquaintances of hers, but also that they were outlaws and robbers who had come to rob her of her bread and kill her. And when at last they caught her and held her, she fought hard against them, showing that even after three days and nights astray, she hadn't weakened at all. It must be mentioned that in Mosfellsdalur, this Guðrún Jónsdóttir was considered a match for a man or more in any test of strength, and in fact, she toppled the men who found her twice before they overcame her there on the heath. Then the farmers led the girl crying across Mosfell Heath until they came down below Bringur, the uppermost farm in Mosfellsdalur, by which time the fog had begun to lift even though the sky was not yet visible.

The girl didn't answer these men when they asked about her wanderings, nor would she accept food from them, saying that over the last three days and nights, she'd drunk her fill of rainwater off of rocks on the heath and wasn't hungry. When they reached the edge of the heath, the sun was shining brightly, and they could see far out over the sea. Little by little, the girl dried out after all those hours of dampness in the drizzly fog, but she had lost her shoes and socks. Now she begins to recognize the men who captured her and sees that they are her neighbors and friends.

The bread that the girl had been sent to fetch was lying there untouched in the wooden bucket.

12

Mosfell Church Receives an Inheritance

Gyra et reversa me per circuitum.[8]

This woman, Guðrún Jónsdóttir from Mosfellsdalur, was known by the inkman now dipping his pen in its inkpot; at that time, he was a milkman, or rather a milk delivery boy, in the above-mentioned community, setting off with milk in pewter cans at four in the morning to sell in the south, while also acting as a substitute in the church choir on Sundays. Even then, that girl had long since grown elderly. Decades later, the same milkman meets the same maid again and asks:

"Wasn't it a bitter pill to swallow, Guðrún, when it looked fairly certain that you would have to spend your life walking in circles on Mosfell Heath?"

The woman then says: "Well, wasn't that what Reverend Jóhann was always trying to preach: turn me around and then turn me around again? I got lost in a fog in the valley on a Wednesday evening, and went south instead of north and then east instead of west."

Question: "Hadn't you given up all hope?"

Answer: "At least I hoped that I wouldn't be prevented from making it in time to hear the priest give the second blessing in Mossvell Church on Sunday."[9]

"Did you make it?" I ask.

"No one made it, alive or dead. The church at Mossvell was torn down those days when I was lost."

"Weren't you a bit frightened?"

"Humph! Why should I have been frightened? There wasn't that much to be frightened of. It couldn't have gotten any darker than it was, at least not then, at the height of spring. I may have felt a bit of a chill the first night because I was soaked to the skin. But the next day I warmed up and laughed at myself for going endlessly in circles. By that evening, I thought I'd lost my mind from all that circling. At sunrise the following morning, a poor, faint little gleam appeared, but quickly disappeared again. So I kept roaming around that day, too. I've never known anyone as dimwitted as me."

Question: "Is it true that you wrote your will in the fog?"

"I really didn't have much of a will to write," says Guðrún Jónsdóttir. "I had three wretched little lambs. That was it. But anyway, on the first night I made a vow to Mossvell Church to give it a lamb if I didn't disgrace myself before God and man by dying of exposure up on a rocky hill in mid-spring."

"Do you think it helped?" I ask.

The woman: "What would it have helped? It didn't help a single thing. Naturally, Mossvell Church wasn't stupid enough to go and buy a lamb from me. The next night I gave Mossvell Church another lamb, without even thinking about getting to hold on to the breath of life in return. Then I started half-expecting that maybe I wouldn't make it home, and how would the poor church know that I'd given it the lambs? If not a word about it was written, and if I never made it home, who would get those blasted little lamb wretches?—because I had no heir. On my last night, I decided to write with my finger on the bare ground: 'The lambs belong to Mossvell Church.' Then I put my initials underneath: 'G. J.' Then I walked up a hill where heather and moss grew and was completely satisfied, because now I'd given all my lambs in writing without expecting ever to get anything in return. I was glad that Mossvell Church should be getting those lamb chits, because it is and will always be my church. And with that, I went to sleep."

Then the lad wanted to know how it came about that the woman took off running and tried to escape when men came and woke her.

"Oh, I was sleeping so well," said the woman. "Never slept better in my life. I was completely out of it, my dear creature. It was a nasty trick they played on me, jolting me from my slumber."

"Was there any truth to it that you tussled with those good friends and neighbors of yours when they finally found you and wanted to bring you home?"

"I wasn't really thinking straight when I woke up," the woman said. "I couldn't recognize the noses on those wretched fellows. Where did you hear this, you poor thing? Who's been peddling such twaddle here in the valley?"

"And you wouldn't even accept coffee and a bite to eat from them, I heard as well."

"Aw, pooh!"

"Weren't you terribly hungry?"

"I don't think a person needs to be eating all the time," said the woman. "It's a bad habit."

Finally, I asked the woman about something that many people have found quite peculiar in this story: why she never broke off a crumb for herself from the loaf of pot bread she carried with her on that long journey night and day through the wilderness. A loaf of bread weighing six pounds should last a person a whole week or even half a month, and longer if it's rationed carefully. The woman was astonished at the absurdities that could stream from the mouth of this youngster; she was close to losing her temper: "You hardly eat what you're entrusted with, dear child."

"You didn't care if you lived or died, as long as the bread made it?" asks the aforementioned milk- and inkman.

“What you’ve been entrusted with, you’ve been entrusted with,” says the woman.

Question: “Can one never be too devoted to one’s master?”

The woman asks in return: “Can one ever be faithful to anyone but oneself?”

“Still, weren’t you glad to be alive when you saw the sun again, Guðrún?”

The woman said that of course a person must be thankful for being allowed to hold on to the breath of life; but one was also thankful for being able to get rid of it. “My great-grandmother had an enormously hard time dying,” she said. “In the end, they had to turn a pot over her head.”

But when the girl was delivered from her endless circling and they reached the edge of the heath, the fog was gone, and the world was there again with the sun and all.

In those days, people used to express themselves more lyrically than now, and I asked the woman if it hadn’t been “wondrous.” I’m afraid she didn’t understand the word. The woman said that as the weather was clearing, she’d been confused for the longest time; what was she doing there with those two men? Suddenly, the world appeared radiant. The fog had lifted. The first thing the girl recognized was the sky. Then she saw the sea far away and knew that was what it was. Then she saw her district, Mosfellsdalur, spreading out as usual below the heath. And finally she recognized the noses on those two fellows. "And before I knew it," says the woman, "I found myself wanting coffee."

The undersigned has often thought about that bread since then—the sort of bread that many a person would want to have. "What happened to the bread?" I ask.

"Oh, I don't really remember," said the maid Guðrún Jónsdóttir, who had become an old woman, pale of cheek. "I suppose it was fed to the horses. The dobbins stood there famished in the farmyard, tail-tied and waiting for the timbers from Mossvell Church to be loaded onto them."

13

Two Names

Due to preoccupation with other topics, this text has so far neglected an account of the rise of Lágafell Church toward Heaven. Despite the fact that Lágafell Church grew taller, however, the superordinates down south were slow to deconsecrate Mosfell Church. Their delay may have worked to strengthen Ólafur of Hrísbrú's faith in the governor and the hope that that particular headman would have it out with the bishop and succeed in bringing "those devils" to their senses. Now there was a serious lack of someone to fight with, and indeed, word went round that Farmer Ólafur raised the issue with Kolbeinn of Kollafjörður, parish council chairman of Mosfell Church, and complained that it was hard to keep holding one's scythe at the ready without having anyone to test its edge on. When he asked whether it wasn't worth attempting to have all those who signed the letter to the governor set fire to the timberwork of Lágafell Church before it was fully built, Kolbeinn of Kollafjörður demurred, considering it to be too late. To Ólafur, the parish council chairman had clearly failed in this matter, like everyone else.

"You are all for yielding but Skammkell," said Farmer Kolbeinn, quoting *Njáll's Saga*.

In reply, Farmer Ólafur cited the same saga, saying that those who ought to have led the prosecution following the burning of Njáll and his sons had no other choice but to seek the support of Mörður Valgarðsson, who had instigated the act—which is why Ólafur of Hrísbrú had come here to see Kolbeinn of Kollafjörður.

"What do you want me to do and say, Ólafur?" asked the parish council chairman.

The farmer replied that he thought it advisable that we, the people of Mosfellsdalur, ask the governor in a new letter if the decrepit old church in Mosfell might continue to stand at our own expense if we so wish; some paltry priest from town could always be hired to bury us, and we would pay him something like fifty aurar per corpse and hot coffee.

This conversation will have led to another letter being sent from the Mosfell parish. This time, the letter was addressed to the district assembly of the Kjalarnes deanery. In it, the parishioners of Mosfell Church ask once again, hoping by the goodwill of the lord bishop over Iceland, that their old and rotten parish church not be completely demolished, God willing, while the old men lived. They also asked that the church authorities not oppose the divine service being held in this church from time to time at the expense of the parishioners of Mosfell, and that the said farmers and their housewives and other members of their households then be allowed to repose in the above- and oft-mentioned poor church's garden of God's children.

The petition in question here, which had evidently originated with Ólafur of Hrísbrú in terms of substance but was perhaps composed and committed to paper by Kolbeinn Eyólfsson, can still be read in a concise summary in the minutes of Kjalarnesþing for the year 1888, as follows: "A letter was presented from the parishioners of the Mosfell parish, requesting that Mosfell Church be allowed to continue to stand and regular church services be conducted there. Two names are signed to the document."

Those two names are not specified in the minutes of the district assembly. Yet in a worn copy of this letter, which certain now-living witnesses recall as having been in their youths, in the possession of an old parishioner, one could still read the names signed to the document, namely:

1. Ólafur Magnússon, Hrísbrú, estate holder.

2. Guðrún Jónsdóttir, Mosfell, maid.

"Guðrún, why did you go and sign that letter along with the late Ólafur of Hrísbrú?"

Guðrún always spoke at the same volume, more suitable for the hard of hearing: "Oh, that old gander once offered me old Bogi, that two-bit son of his, and I half felt as if I should do something for him in return, although I would rather have died than be enslaved to old Bogi of Hrísbrú, or any other so-called man."

"And what did your priest, Reverend Jóhann, say when he returned from the deans' meeting and saw that you had signed a document against him?"

Guðrún Jónsdóttir, answer: "He said, 'two is always two'—then he points at himself and says: 'Here is the one who stands for the third. But the third never signs. He's just there.'"

Question: "Who was he talking about?"

G. J. "Reverend Jóhann never talked with anyone about anything except the man in the sky. When he talked to people, he was always talking about the man in the sky. Even when he talked with the madam, he was talking about the man in the sky; nor did he have long to wait before being made priest of the cathedral down south. But in fact, he resigned from the priesthood temporarily that spring because the missus was ill. Reverend Jóhann never went to Lágafell, despite his plans for a cheap churchyard there. He went to Copenhagen to seek medical treatment for the madam, until she died."

Question: "Didn't he say anything, either, when he heard that on top of the letter to the deans, you had bequeathed your lambs to Mosfell Church?"

G. J. "No lout of a man in Moskó has ever given less of a shit concerning where the church stood as Reverend Jóhann.[10] He gave me a gold coin when he said goodbye to me."

Question: "Of course he was delighted when you made it back with the bread untouched?"

G. J. "Reverend Jóhann?! Oh, phooey. As if he would have been pleased—or the opposite!" (N.B., she never used the word "delighted.") "Reverend Jóhann only said 'Give us this day our daily bread,' and then gave the bread to the horses. So I say to Reverend Jóhann, just like this, what a brilliant idea—or not!—giving that ragamuffin Big Gunna a gold coin. What would pitiful Mókolla me want with a gold coin?[11]

"Reverend Jóhann then says, 'I have only this one gold coin. It's for you. If I ever get another one, I'm going to give it to you, too, my dear Guðrún. But I doubt that God will ever send me more than this one gold coin.'"

14

No Bell Found

Three carpenters from the south tore down Mosfell Church with their crowbars. They stacked the debris along with the church's chattel outside the lychgate. The work was completed in a single day, from six in the morning to three in the afternoon. No formal remarks were made before the church was taken from its children. Not even the two people who had signed the last letter were present. One God-fearing man is said to have stated that the Redeemer had rarely seen so much trouble taken to raze such a poor church to the ground. Why couldn't it just be left to wear away in the wind? There were also those who said that since the church hadn't been deconsecrated, it would go on standing as before on a hill in the homefield of Heaven. Some wags wrote the following verses on this topic:

Midst Heaven's fields so famed and fair
Mosfell Church stands on high hill.
The morning sun its smile meets there
where all is sweetly dry and still.

Lithely three lambs their cuds chew
with Heaven's homefield as their bed.
Gifted there by Guðrún, who
tends so well unto her bread.

To continue quoting this woman, she told me that all the then-living men of any moxie here in the valley naturally wanted Mosfell Church and absolutely none other. From some, the church fee had to be collected by distraint each year after the church was moved to Lágafell—as well as the associated burial fee. "Many never went to church after Mossvell Church was torn down," said Big Guðrún, "and until they were carried into Lágafell Church in a shroud and out again into an unfamiliar churchyard. One or two started buying the magazine *The Seed* from the Adventists. I knew of some who betook themselves to Mossvell in good weather on a summer's evening, went up the hill and sat down in the churchyard and read the old stones, especially the slab of the late Reverend Magnús Grímsson, the poet, a former priest at Mossvell, whose inscription was so beautiful; it was he who published the story of Snow White and the Seven Dwarfs, which is so lovely. When I was there, moss had already started to grow over the letters, so you had to scratch the words with your fingernails to read them. The entire stone has long since been covered by moss, but I know where it is," said Guðrún. "It was he who delivered the eulogy for those Easterners who were traveling to the fishing station and died of exposure on Mossvell Heath at Christmas during the Great Christmas Storm. I have it written down because I always feel like it's my heath."

Question: "If everyone had signed along with you and old Ólafur of Hrísbrú and everyone had threatened to go to war, wouldn't the bishop have given in, especially since the governor had softened his stance?"

G. J. "Oh, I don't think they would have done much warring, those wets, not a shred of virility among those blasted wretches but Ólafur of Hrísbrú. He wanted to fight like a man, the old codger. He just couldn't find anyone to fight against him, and in fact had no one at his side but his poor old son Bogi, who only had a rake. Everyone was praying and hoping that there'd be war, but that was as far as doughtiness went in these parts."

Now, many people might think that this story was over and done with and that the aforementioned church had been moved to the green fields of Heaven for good. But far from it. The story is still only half told. Now the real story begins.

In the spring of 1888, someone asks out of the blue: "What ever became of the churchbell at Mosfell? No bell was found in the junk carried out onto the hill along with the church timbers." The carpenters were asked if one of them had taken down the bell. They hadn't tampered with any bell, they said. Now the cross-examination began: "So maybe there was no bell?"

First carpenter: "Sure there was a bell."

Second carpenter: "Well, I really don't remember. There was most likely a bell. Or there just was no bell."

Third carpenter: "I'm buggered if I saw any goddamn bell there."

After a bit more prodding, all three men began contradicting themselves, changing their statements over and over. Finally, each of them had spoken for and against all conceivable possibilities in this matter and declared under oath that there had both been and not been a bell.

New question: "But the chalice and that other stuff?"

Answer: "One other would know."

Question: "Well, and who would that one other be?"

"Were people so foul-mouthed in those days?" asks the person who was speaking to G. J.

Guðrún Jónsdóttir: "Those miserable runts always went on like that, as if it helped grow themselves a pair because they aren't real men."

Finally, it came to light that Reverend Jóhann had wrapped the chasuble and surplice around the altarpiece, the candelabra, and the paten and sent the parcel to the late Reverend Þórarinn at Garðar; Reverend Jóhann kept the cassock because it belonged to him. Now Dean Þórarinn sends a message that the chalice was not among the things sent to him. Where was the chalice?

Ólafur of Hrísbrú then told Kolbeinn of Kollafjörður, when this matter came up: "It was only to be expected of those devils that they would end up stealing Mosfell Church's inventory. But I can well understand how Reverend Jóhann, arch-robber that he is, wouldn't stoop so low as to steal such a saucer as that paten."

Whatever may have happened to the chalice, it was common knowledge in the district that the night after Mosfell Church was demolished, Reverend Jóhann handed over its bell to Ólafur of Hrísbrú and suggested that he give it a tap or two to pass the time when he was bored. I'm not sure if I buy this story, but it is certainly possible that Reverend Jóhann, for the love of God, turned a blind eye in this matter as he did in many others.

15

A Trifle

The authorities never took formal action in the disappearance of the sacred objects, as was now described, apparently considering it more trouble than it was worth to blow excessively from an official direction on smoke that was already billowing high enough in the district. For example, there was no organized search for thieves. At one point, it was heard whispered that good men had been advised by even better men to keep their eyes peeled if they happened to pass through the yards of certain farms in the old Mosfell parish. Most apparently just narrowed one eye and left it at that; after all, one couldn't expect respectable men to want to be seen as the sort who would snoop around for sacred objects in their neighbors' manure gutters.

In Iceland, a priest's benefice, his living, is called his bread, as it provides him his sustenance. Now that their church had fallen and the Mosfell bread was erased from the number of existing ones, with no word of God to be heard there from then on into eternity, people thought of their bell like the farmer whose flock had all been washed off a skerry, apart from one unhorned russet ewe; the farmer took this sheep and hurled it into the sea after the other ones, remarking as he did that it would be better off with the devil, too.

Now the days passed uneventfully and people forget Mosfell Church along with the bell and chalice in the lethargy induced by the healing hands of time. The same thing had occurred many centuries earlier, in papist times, when the oft-mentioned church was taken from its parishioners and its heathlands were made the mountain pastures of the sheep of Þerney Church in Sund, among other such tricks. And finally, when the Redeemer returned to his senses and gave them back Mosfell Church, a different faith had come to the country and there were no longer any saints but the Danish king and Luther. Everyone had forgotten which saint it was who owned this church originally, but many believed it to have been Egill Skallagrímsson.

We shall now return to the conversation that the inkman had many years later with the maid, Big Guðrún Jónsdóttir, who had by then become a pauper.

Yes, back in the day she would often go from farm to farm on her 'plug mare'; the whole district was her home.

"No, I never left the valley, except for once, to attend a funeral down south," she said. Her preferred jobs were washing wool, boiling cow's urine, and mucking out sheep sheds in the spring. And of course, there was helping out with the butchering in the autumn, bloody up to her elbows, in addition to haymaking, a week here and a week there as needed to give a hand to those sorry sheeplings, but she only ever mowed; never touched a rake.

When she said "sorry sheeplings" she meant people in general, like you and me and ones that she liked—up to a point. "Always invited and welcomed by those pitiful wretches, yes, indeed! I never felt comfortable unless it was a darned hard slog. No, never hired on as a domestic. Never paid a wage. Suited only for filthy jobs. Liked it best in peat pits, when no one ever saw you and you wound up looking not a whit human. You got soaked to the bone from all that good, pure muck. Or the blessed stench of freshly cut peat! It's the most fun I know. And it wasn't too shabby, the smoke from dry peat in the winter, if it was good peat."

Question: "Did you never want a husband?"

"Never cozied up to any man. Hahaha. Was one of the king's freewomen, as they're called, and had a letter to that effect, though some say it was useless; maybe fake. Had only a chestnut mare to sit on."

I don't think I ever heard this nun use the word "mare" on its own except for that one time; she always said "the nag," "the jade," or "the bag o' bones." Sometimes her "plug mare." On this mare, the woman traveled around her world and did unpaid odd jobs; arranged astride the horse's back were her thin duvet and bag holding her Sunday-best cardigan and a copy of *Meditations* by the Reverend Pétur Pétursson, Doctor of Theology and Bishop of Iceland, who had Mossvell Church demolished. She would sometimes read haltingly from this on Sunday afternoons, rocking in her seat. Guðrún Jónsdóttir never blamed anyone who had taken the church from her. But when I asked her how she liked Pétur Pétursson's *Meditations*, she gave a little shrug and said, "Aw, he's damned soulless." When I spoke to the woman, her mare had been dead for over a quarter of a century. Still, that mare was one of the most vivid, living-breathing ones ever told of, and I imagined her as pregnant almost all the time.

G. J. often passed by Hrísbrú, where the men would be lined up on the pavestones outside the door, but she was never asked to do any work there, she said, and she wouldn't have married a member of that household even if it would have cost her her life to refuse. But she always enjoyed bantering with those cussed geezers, who stood there like piss pots on the bone-dry pavestones and exchanged words with passersby whose horses were up to their bellies in the mire out front.

"Well, in any case, once as so often before I was making my way through the Hrísbrú farmyard on my Chestnut and the men are up there on the pavestones as usual. Before I know it, that rascal, the late Ólafur, says 'Hello there.' But he wasn't in the habit of blathering to visitors, was the late Ólafur. 'Fimmbjörg,' says the man, because he always said Fimmbjörg; 'Fimmbjörg was saying the other day that Big Gunna should come in here the next time she passed by.'"

Guðrún Jónsdóttir says that she thought that a bit strange. Ever since she was a sprout, she said, she'd been passing by the place and had never once been invited in. As a result, she'd never seen the late Finnbjörg. How could that bedridden old dame know that a person like her, called by everyone "Big Gunna," existed? Shouldn't that tuckered-out grandame have had something more important to think about than this Big Gunna—especially having been lying on the brink of death for eighteen years. (NB, in that district, the number of years that Finnbjörg was said to have been bedridden was always eighteen; they never increased or decreased despite the woman's time in bed being lengthened by a year each year.)

"Well, in any case, the men tell me I should watch out for the slough in front of the farm door, which is said to be an ancient quagmire and was supposedly where they splashed the contents of their night pots in the time of the Sturlungs. I'm not convinced of that. In any case, when you got in past that bottomless pit and were out of mortal danger, then you started to feel your way through those pitch-dark earthen tunnels with their eighteen turns—although naturally, the homefolk found their way in and out of that bastard as if in broad daylight—until you came to a slamming door that slammed shut on its own—without a slam—by means of a loom-stone hanging on a string. And then I found myself in the family room, where, people said, no one was ever invited in."

Now Guðrún Jónsdóttir explains that after emerging from those cursed, blasted, long and crooked passageways, you find yourself in a family room divided into three: two spaces with earthen floors between partition posts, the floors so glossy smooth that not a speck of dirt could be seen on them, while the outermost space, nearest the gable window, had a platform floor, whereupon the woman's bed stood under the sloping ceiling; daylight fell over her left shoulder as she lay there half erect, knitting.

"So, there she lay in her bed, the poor woman, where she'd lain for eighteen years, that piteous creature—and hardly a surprise, considering she was married to the late Ólafur—or, better put, she sat up in the light and endeavored to knit a shawl." Guðrún Jónsdóttir said that the woman looked at her familiarly and laid her knitting needles on the sill above her, ". . . and then she says to me, just like this, and she needn't have done so at all, the blessed woman, 'Hello, dear Gunna, and welcome.' 'Thank you kindly,' I say. It was as if we were old friends and hadn't seen each other for a year. I'll be blowed if I saw anything wrong with the old woman; bugger me if she was any more crippled than me, apart from her fingers being slightly more crooked than mine from that confounded knit-poking of hers. I didn't see her legs, though; hers may have been frail, but mine weren't. But to me her cheeks looked surprisingly smooth, for being married to the departed Ólafur; she seemed much younger than those rascal sons of hers. She wasn't exactly the most exuberant of manner, the old dear; there was nothing hasty or rash about her. But she was amiable, the poor thing, and her words carried weight. Maybe she'd gone through something difficult in her past that had lately become easier to bear. It was like being in the presence of an elf woman. And then she calls to her daughter Gunsa, who was going to get married down in Suðurnes, and says to her, quick now, bring some coffee water, because it was early-evening coffee time; and Gunsa returns with genuine cream coffee, by God, in a rosy cup, just like the hidden people have. She herself reached into the chest in front of her and took out the sugar, and I tell you, she wasn't serving up that tooth-cracking rock sugar, but real melis like Reverend Jóhann got on Sundays. It's not so often that something so good falls into my lap. Yet that was only the beginning, because then came the piping hot flannel-cakes, thick and hearty and so sweet and succulent that you practically drooled eating them, no, they definitely weren't your usual bone-hard wholemeal cookies. You wouldn't think you were in the Mossvell district. They made me think of the good old outlaw dwellings in the Ódáðahraun lava wastes that we were told stories about as kids.

"So then I say this to the woman, 'Almighty, you're chipper now!'

"'I'm getting by,' says the woman.

"'And taking the right medicines, no question about that,' I say.

"'And so far, I haven't had to resort to old Fúsi's sheep-dung treatment. On the other hand, I'm always reciting verses by Reverend Jón Þorláksson of Bæsá, my great-uncle.'

G. J. 'Yes, it always makes a difference knowing a good verse, I say; especially if you recite it at the right time. And it looks to me as if you'll soon be on your feet again.'"

The woman has nothing to say to that, but after a moment, remarks to the girl: "'It's no wonder if it surprises you that a person like me should be inviting folk in.'

G. J. 'Well, you hit the nail on the head there, my dear lady—if you're counting Big Gunna as *folk* now!'

"The woman no longer listened to fiddle-faddle or the sort of blather bandied only for the sake of appearances; instead, she starts speaking as elf women used to do when they had important things to say to people here in the past: 'I have always kept my eye on you, Little Guðrún, ever since you were a girl. Now I shall recite a verse for you, and you must learn it and repeat it to yourself should you ever be confined to your sickbed.'"

The inkman asks Guðrún (forty years later): "Did you learn the verse?"

G. J. "Aw, I'm damned if I did. And yet."

Question: "Was it a good verse?"

G. J. "Aw, it was some cussed, woe-is-me bleating from that rascal up north. Poets are always whining about how the world isn't good enough for them, and that's because they don't work in peat pits. Hopefully I'll start understanding poetry once I'm bedridden. But the verses will have to be a bit cheerful, like, for example, Gröndal's verse about the old fellow at Spónsgerði."

Now the Hrísbrú woman goes on whispering as the elf women did, saying to the girl: "'I've heard that you can be safely entrusted with certain little things.'"

"'That hasn't been put much to the test,' Guðrún Jónsdóttir says was her reply, and she never lowered her voice when others whispered, but kept it at its usual volume.

"Finnbjörg goes on whispering: 'I hope and pray constantly that I be allowed to go. This has dragged on long enough, I think. I don't have the strength for it anymore. I stopped recognizing myself a long time ago. It wasn't much; now it's over. But I have a little something here in my keeping.'

"Now the woman starts rooting around in her bed beneath the headboard and finally finds some apparatus tied up in a headcloth of glossy black silk. It was the sort of soft, supple silk that smooths out readily after it's wrinkled, and came here with the ships in the past—not like the humbug and flimflam stuff being imported now. And what should happen then but that the numb-fingered woman pulls out the chalice from Mossvell Church—nothing less!"

When Guðrún Jónsdóttir was asked if she was certain that it was the right chalice and whether it could just as well have been the wrong chalice, she was taken aback and answered hotly: "How often as a kid didn't I fall asleep staring at that bloody contraption standing there on the altar during mass, glinting in the sunlight?! I even drank from it when I was confirmed. Yes, and there it was again, that blasted thing, right in front me, as I live and breathe!"

Guðrún goes on and the inkman writes: "Somehow that poor old dear had gotten it into her head that the only wretch in Mossvellsdalur who didn't have even a lousy old chest with its own little casket, let alone anything to put into a chest or keep in its little casket, this muttonhead, I say, should now start keeping valuables and covering up for thieves, yes, who'd even stolen from a church, which is double thievery, and for which one must answer both to the sheeplings here and the old man up in the sky. 'You've got a screw loose, Finnbjörg,' I say, 'if you think I'm going to lay my paws on that miserable old figure work there. I'd be called before the magistrate. They'd toss me in the clink. And who would look after that chalice rubbish when I was locked up? Kolbeinn of Kollafjörður and the bigwigs here would of course stroll straightaway with it over to Lágafell Church.'

"'The old man in the sky has certainly seen more than a few people like our Kolbeinn and the bigwigs here,' says Housewife Finnbjörg.

"'For me, it's out of the question,' says Guðrún Jónsdóttir. 'I'm not coming any-bloody-where near it. All the tussocks here in Mossvellsdalur can sooner hop to Heaven and all the hollows sink to Hell, so help me.'

"'This silk cloth should go with it,' says Finnbjörg Finnsdóttir. 'It belonged to my dear departed grandmother, who was the sister of the national poet at Bæsá, the deceased Reverend Jón Þorláksson.'"

Here, Guðrún Jónsdóttir takes a pinch of snuff as a signal that her narrative is finished.

I, the undersigned, felt that the story of these two women of our district, who spoke to each other only once and never since, needed something more by way of closure. They were truly in a world of their own, these women. I waited and waited, but nothing more came.

"You forgot to end your story," I finally say. "How did it go?"

"Go? It didn't go anywhere. It went as it went. Naturally, I took the chalice."

Question: "And are you going to keep it for the rest of your life?"

"I suppose the one who owns it will have no trouble retrieving it when he sees fit," replied this Guðrún Jónsdóttir.

16

The Episode of the Transport Man Begins

Now the story turns to the south, as folk in the Mosfell district say when they mean the capital.

Once upon a time, there was a small half-stone house, hardly more than a man's height up to the gable, in the corner of a kitchen garden at the intersection of Bergstaðastígur Street and Baldursgata Street just above Vassmýri, where the tern lives.[12] There was a small rock wall maybe knee-high around the kitchen garden, in which grew chickweed. At the back was the water barrel. This was the house of Shorty-Láki, who was called Ash-Láki when others spoke of him, but Láki when they spoke to him, and Þorlákur in official documents.

Láki, who lived there, was a man of slight build. He lived alone. Somehow, he owned this little half-stone house. The house had both a vestibule, filled with boxes, and a kitchen, where there was a rather sooty oil stove that smelled of kerosene. Farther in was the meager little room where Láki slept.

Not everyone was loaded with money in those days, and back then, both the 25-aurar coins and even the 10-aurar ones were made of silver. Yet no one was called poor unless he was dependent on poor relief due to being an invalid or at least insane. Láki, on the other hand, was an independent man because he had created his own means of employment. He put together a wheelbarrow of the kind invented by the Chaldeans a few centuries after they invented astrology, and in this wheelbarrow he carried away people's ashes, etc. He picked up the ashes from people's back doors and drove them staidly, almost solemnly, down to Vassmýri, where he dumped them from the wheelbarrow onto a pile prescribed by the town authorities. Built on that same site later were the University of Iceland and its associated cultural institutions, with many more yet to come. It cost 25 aurar per house to drive away the ashes, 10 aurar for small loads. The driver took payment in cash. He kept every coin wrapped in its own little piece of paper so they wouldn't get scratched. He got up at five in the morning and often worked late into the evening. He was skinny as a stick, despite having enough rye bread that he got from the bakery for carting away its ashes, while old fishermen he knew gave him fish at the seashore.

I never heard of anyone having words with this man, but young scamps shouted at him: "Hey hey Shorty-Láki, ha ha Ash-Láki!" Fortunately, he seemed to have been hard of hearing. And what do you know?—apparently, he got together with a woman when, just for fun, he spent part of one summer doing day labor in Kjalarnes. The man hasn't yet been born in Iceland who hasn't found a woman suitable for him, because all people, both women and men, are each and every one born into this world by the mercy of God. This woman's name was Sólrún and she was from the country's north. Few people had heard of this adventure of Ash-Láki's, yet eventually, rumor flew that he was the father of a boy up north, namely in Eyjafjörður, whence the great poets come.

Now time passes, and soon it will have been six years since the summer when Shorty-Láki went up to Kjalarnes. Then, one fine day, it so happens that a Poor Law Guardian leads a small boy by the hand to the little half-stone house on the aforewritten street corner; they have come to speak to Þorlákur. No one was home, so the Guardian sat down on the low rock wall and waited there with the boy until the householder returned. The boy was five years old. He was wearing a jacket suited to a far larger man, and inside the jacket was sewn a letter signed and stamped by authorities in distant parts of the country. The letter stated that this boy was the son of Þorlákur, a transport man in Reykjavík, and a woman from the north, named Sólrún, who was dead.

The Board of Guardians in Eyjafjörður had sent this little boy on his own from administrator to administrator in over twenty districts, over high mountain ranges, valleys, heaths, and unbridged rivers. The journey took half a year, one short stretch at a time, with constantly changing traveling companions, few being in any position to look after a living child for more than a short distance. Thus did the boy continue his journey: always new mountains and new valleys, one new river after another, a new resting place each night, foul weather, district administrators; it was as if the world were endless. But now that long journey was done. The traveler is sitting there on a rock wall along with a district administrator in the south, and has come home.

Finally his father returned, pushing his wheelbarrow ahead of him. He immediately acknowledged the boy as his son and signed his name to a paper handed him by the Poor Law Guardian, but was saddened to hear that the boy's mother was dead. His business having been concluded, the Guardian went home, while Ash-Láki took his son by the hand and led him into the house.

17

Raising Shark

At that time an open stream flowed through our capital, and was called the Stream; in it were sticklebacks. Occasionally, you could see an eel there, too, migrating from the Sargasso Sea to a pond, called the Pond, located behind the Alþingi House and the cathedral. By his own later account, the northerner told of in the preceding chapter busied himself during his first year in the capital with catching sticklebacks and sometimes an eel by hand at the Pond.

As mentioned earlier, his father got up at five o'clock each morning and pushed his famous wheelbarrow, which, according to the theory of evolution, the Chaldeans invented in continuation of astrology. By the time Stefán Þorláksson woke in the morning, his father had long since gone out. But there was always a bit of rye bread, sometimes dried out and sometimes moldy, in the kitchen. Sometimes there was also half-dried lumpfish and a bite of cured skate, both of which emit an odor unknown in Iceland's north. Often, there was also a bucket of water. There was no one to talk to when Stefán woke up in the morning. Elsewhere, he had neither friends nor others to chat with, except for a few bigger boys on their way to school, who yelled "Hey hey, ha ha" at Stebbi Shorty-Láki's son. So he had no other company but those strange fish from the Stream. Soon, however, he found the path down to the seashore and watched the fishermen return with fish of various colors and shapes, some large, including a shark, which happens not to be unknown to the folk in the north. The boy was very fond of these fish because they were the only ones he'd seen in the north and in fact the only creature, not excluding humans, that he recognized here in the south.

It was mentioned earlier that his father had an old barrel that collected rainwater from a gutter on the roof of the small half-stone house, which gave the boy the idea of producing shark in the barrel. His common sense told him that this would be possible by catching eels from the Stream and raising them in the barrel. In his view, the eels were so slender because they had too little to eat in the Pond—no other fish are found there. So he put sticklebacks in the barrel along with the eels, expecting that if an eel ate enough sticklebacks it would eventually become a shark or at least as portly as a shark. Then he would sell the shark and buy himself new shoes with the money he earned.

Unfortunately, the sticklebacks died before their time in the barrel and the eels died as well, so there were never any sharks. Nor shoes, either.

His father habitually stopped carting ashes at six o'clock every Saturday. He would then come home. He would bring his son a cornet of candies and frequently two types of sweet breads, one called "Sturla bread" because it was bought in Sturla Jónsson's store, while the other was called "letter bread" because it came in pieces that were shaped like letters and no bigger than a fingernail. Sturla bread was rock-hard and a little sweet, whereas letter bread was crispy and airy inside, and not really sweet even though it was sold as such. Þorlákur had heard that the children of better-placed parents learned to read by eating this bread.

Sometimes he walked hand-in-hand with his son to church on Sunday mornings, but wouldn't bring him along when he was carting ashes, feeling it too flippant to involve his children in the responsible duty of carting away the ashes of distinguished persons in the community. The one scribbling all this down now remembers the late ashman, Þorlákur, quite well. He was the spitting image of the late Michelangelo Buonarroti; I think everyone who has had any reason to compare them would agree.

In the winter it was sometimes cold in Þorlákur's house; the stream was frozen, the sticklebacks weren't there, and the eels had gone to the great depths of the Sargasso Sea, as Stefán

Þorláksson told the person writing this. The boy caught a cold and lay in bed for much of the winter, until his father managed to get him a decoction of Iceland moss from a fortune teller out on Seltjarnarnes. His father was busy all Christmas straightening bent, rusty nails. Stefán Þorláksson said that he couldn't recall there having been much sun that winter, either. Yet in the end, that celestial body started peeking through Láki's window, as it sometimes does in the north. Finally, finally. Then the tern arrived and screeched sleepily in Vassmýri. A pale boy crawled out of bed and went down to the Stream to check on his friends the sticklebacks and eels; and they started arriving, too. But no shark ever came of it, as told of before.

18

Houseguest at Hrísbrú

Now the story turns once more to Mosfellsdalur, the parish that we left earlier, after the benefice there was dissolved and the church leveled to the ground, and everyone long since having started to think about more pressing matters. Yet although times change, the autumn rains in that district never do. And most wearisome are the southeasterlies with their ever-present gusts. I don't recall if I've mentioned it before, but in that district, the seasons and weather are gauged with regard to sheep, not people. It had been a rather bad autumn for sheep. At this point in the story, it was around time for the final sheep sorting, and not too long afterward, the lambs would be brought into their sheds and fed hay there. It was wetter and muddier now at Hrísbrú, where the road leads north. The wind blew against the window of the late Finnbjörg as she knitted by dim lantern light, which burned even when all other lights in the valley were extinguished. The lads were securing the doors for the night, what with the rain and wind pressing in from that direction.

In the midst of this storm, something living happens to be scrambling along the road where it meets the path to the house. In short, this creature makes it through the mud and up onto the walkway, where it sits down on the doorstone in the rain, right in the gleam coming from Finnbjörg's family-room window.

Although the father and his sons were of course not very keen-sighted in daylight, they could see surprisingly well in the dark. Now, as far as they could tell, crawling up from the mire out front came a young lad of smallish stature, hardly bigger than Írafellsmóri, who had long been the most famous character and most prominent ghost in the countryside around Mount Esja, although he doesn't figure in these meager pages.

Ólafur's sons say to their father: "Someone has come."

"Is it a man?" asks Ólafur.

"It doesn't appear otherwise," they say.

Although, at that time, the late Ólafur could barely see well enough to pee in daylight, as he himself said, his sons trusted him better than anyone to discern the difference between a man and a ghost in the dark, and asked him to decide on this matter. Farmer Ólafur steps out onto the pavestones and asks:

"Where have you come from in this weather, chum?"

"I've come from the south," answers a little boy.

"And where are you going?" they ask.

"I'm going north," said the boy.

"In whose charge are you?" they ask.

"Sólrún's," said the boy.

"And who is Sólrún?" they said.

"She's dead," said the boy.

"How far north are you going?" they say.

"To Eyjafjörður," said the boy.

"You know the way to Eyjafjörður?"

"Yes," said the boy.

"Aren't you afraid?" they said.

"Yes," said the boy.

"Don't you know that it's a journey of fourteen days by pack train north to Eyjafjörður?" they ask.

"I don't have a pack train," said the boy.

"The route crosses the worst rivers in the country."

"That doesn't matter," said the boy. "I've had to wade three times today."

"Weren't our rivers here in this district, Kaldaklofslækur and Kortúlstaðá, deep enough for you?"

"No," the boy said, "they only came up to my neck."

Then Farmer Ólafur asks: "What are you afraid of, chum, if it's not wading in water up to your neck?"

"I stole Ash-Láki's sou'wester," replies the boy. "I was so afraid of people I met on the road recognizing me."

"You thought you'd get a spanking, huh?" said the men of Hrísbrú.

The boy said: "I turned my hat around on my head. I had the back facing forward so no one would recognize me."

Then he goes on with the story of his journey: "The path lay over a terribly long, stony hill, and I got scared again. I ran as fast as I could. I fell and fell. There was no house. No person. No animal. I thought robbers would come and attack me. But I escaped. Then I got scared for the third time. It was getting dark and the path lay along the foot of a terribly big mountain. I thought the mountain would tumble down on top of me. I couldn't help but run the whole way from the path down to the sea so I wouldn't be under the mountain when it crumbled."

Previously, it was mentioned that the folk at Hrísbrú weren't in the habit of asking strangers how things were with them, even if they happened to be passing through the farmyard. For some reason, they broke their habit that night. The late Ólafur, who had little interest in where others bedded down for the night, even says this to the traveler:

"Where are you thinking of staying tonight?"

"I don't know," said the boy.

"Have you had anything to eat?" says Farmer Ólafur.

"Yes, yes," says the boy.

"When?" asks Farmer Ólafur.

"The other day," said the boy.

"The other day? What blasted day?" asks the farmer.

"I don't really remember," said the boy.

Then Ólafur says to his sons: "Don't lose him to the wind and rain while I pop in and ask Fimmbjörg."

After a short spell, the late Ólafur felt his way back to the front door and invited Stefán Þorláksson to stay the night.

He stayed there for twenty years.

19

The New Fróðá Marvels

It would be a useful man who could write the story of Stefán Þorláksson, but the inkman at work here doesn't have what it takes to do so. As soon as this houseguest came to Hrísbrú, a new line appeared in the face of the district: the boy who wanted to produce shark in a barrel. He was the leaven that heralded traffic and competition in this bread.

Stefán Þorláksson was always trading knives, which the men of Hrísbrú never did. He acquired all sorts of knives, starting by swapping like for like, but then trying to get a big knife for a small one or two for one. Once he came home with a machete for his foster father Ólafur so that he could go to battle, but Farmer Ólafur said that he no longer had the sight for fighting and told the boy to take it to Finnbjörg. The woman sent the weapon to the kitchen and said that it would be useful for cutting fish.

When Stefán was confirmed, they gave him a pipe but no tobacco. He found it a strange gift, but Finnbjörg said that more people had died from tobacco smoke than that of hay leavings and peat, which has always led to the most unbreathable air in Iceland. The boy understood this woman, despite her offering guidance in a rather roundabout way, and it has been said of this houseguest that throughout his life, he never put any stock in any other person's advice. He would laugh at most of what others said, and because of it, was considered a lighthearted man, but he kept Finnbjörg's wishes close to his heart all his life, and said of his foster mother that she'd been so far ahead of others that though they climbed the highest hill, they would but glimpse her in the distance. Once he got his pipe, he abstained from tobacco and never touched it his entire life; on the other hand, he acquired nine tobacco pipes after a week (eighteen, legend has it).

He was given a colt and waited one winter for it to become a horse. In the autumn, he attended the Kollafjörður sheep-sorting to separate out the Hrísbrú sheep, being sharp-eyed when it came to earmarks. Yet despite already having more than enough on his plate that day, he did find time to do some horse trading. When he returned home, it turned out that he'd given away his horse, but brought back three in its place: a brood mare and its suckling foal, and an adult packhorse, as well.

At that time, the first automobiles were being imported into the country, introducing new marvels to this nation of farmers who had worked with the same implements since the year 900—around the time of the bizarre, wondrous manifestations called the Fróðá Marvels.[13] Soon, surrounded by these new, uncanny inventions, no farmer recognized himself any longer, and the poets began lamenting their loss of identity in print. One fine day, Stefán drives a car that he himself owned up to the homefield wall at Hrísbrú and parks it there, not trusting it in the mire out front of the farmhouse. Cars that came to this country back then were apparently rattletraps, at first, having been transported from Canada, where they'd seen far better days. Once here, they stopped running, particularly on thoroughfares. Their drivers walked backwards pushing these vehicles up hills, down which they'd immediately roll, in keeping with the law of gravity. Yet everyone admired automobiles and began to believe in them—Stefán Þorláksson the most. For many people, they replaced Írafellsmóri and those poor old sheep and schnapps; for some they replaced the identity they'd lost. It was thought a great idea to drive a car on Sundays from Reykjavík all the way east to Þingvellir, 50 kilometers, to buy a bottle of belch water.

Stefán traded his horses and other possessions for a car and, for several years now, was always out on the roads, despite his domicile and refuge being at Hrísbrú. He drove people from one place to another, sometimes for money. He experimented with using kerosene instead of gasoline, the result being a beautiful blue exhaust accompanied by strange pops and churnings in the engine. Sometimes, after the car had stood unmoving for a while up on Mosfell Heath, sophisticated belch-water folk would suddenly turn up and offer their help, holding a flaming match to Stefi's gas tank; but since the car didn't blow up immediately, they concluded that it was out of gas. So one of them was sent to try to buy gas somewhere, or at least borrow kerosene. One Ford on such an outing to Þingvellir, with blue smoke trailing behind it, made more of a racket than the combined Ford factories in Detroit. Often a driver had to stay on the heath for days at a time while tinkering with his car's engine. There are Icelandic poems from those days about people who'd become entangled in their engines like philosophers in their systems (and one could perhaps add nowadays: like idealogues in their universal theories).

Stefi Shorty-Lákason, as the kids called him, became as famous early on for Fordianism as others for Freudianism and various progressive views of life that were starting to take hold at the time. But then he himself said that although Ólafur at Hrísbrú and his sons snorted at the strange bird that had crawled out of its egg among them, they were impressed by him and loved him as a brother born in monstrous form, perhaps with two heads, and whom you mustn't kick because you don't understand God's ways. The Hrísbrú folk never blamed Stefán even if it took him three days to go east to Þingvellir to buy himself a bottle of belch water and he had to spend the nights on the heath with his car. It was as if those ancients sensed that the strange visitor who showed up at their door one autumn evening and introduced traffic and competition to the district had come to stay.

Concerning Stefán Þorláksson's schooling, there isn't much to write. He grew up before today's compulsory education was legislated. Prior to his confirmation, he was sent along with several other children in the same situation to the farmer at Laxnes to learn their catechism and Bible stories, along with arithmetic up to the rule of three and fractions and to study the map in the *Book of Þórarinn* showing the world split in two like a sheep's head prepared for boiling.

Christianity wasn't practiced at Hrísbrú, although Finnbjörg apparently had a collection of sermons that she rarely read and never talked about. Those people's Christianity had always consisted of going to church; they thought it useless to read about God in a book, and even more senseless now that their church had been razed to the ground. Stefán couldn't recall prayers and things of that sort during his upbringing after he stopped going to church with Láki in the south; Christianity was of little concern to him, it being impossible to change, anyway, if it happened to be wrong. Sometimes Finnbjörg recited a poem by the late Reverend Jón at Bæsá, but Stefán didn't pay much attention and she never tried to teach it to him; after all, some of what that fellow wrote wasn't quite up to par, Stefán said, before reciting the verse "I Pounce on Everything in Front of Me," which he'd learned from other drivers, and not from his foster mother. On the other hand, she taught her foster boy how to knit socks so that he would have something for his hands to do if he went blind. She had him sit next to her and helped him if he dropped a stitch. Otherwise, by his own admission, Stefán never heard of anything supernatural in Mosfellsdalur during the twenty years that he was there, apart from the aforementioned ghost from Írafell in Kjós. This ghost frequently came over Svínaskarð Pass in the depths of winter, especially during snowstorms. On some farms in the area around Mount Esja, a bit of food was put out for him on top of the farmhouse wall in the evenings, but not at Hrísbrú, although the folk there sometimes got the feeling that he was lurking in the passageways or between buildings at twilight. Finnbjörg refused to allow a bowl of food to be left up on the wall for the ghost, saying that stray dogs or feral cats would gulp it down at night; she didn't want to attract any vagrant varmints to the place.

Stefán said that he most regretted having forgotten to ask the woman anything during the three or four years that he'd had the opportunity to sit by her sickbed, except for some trifles about knitting. Was she really ill?—this question, he said, he'd often asked himself later. Or maybe everyone was ill but her? Those innumerable women in Iceland who lay bedridden for eighteen years, was there anything wrong with them apart from being too strong to take part in the misery and stupidity that everyone else in this country took for granted and consoled themselves with or even rejoiced in, like beggars and their boils? He said that the air of modesty, composure, and purity that emanated from that woman he had later sought but never found in any other woman, despite having driven incessantly all over the country his whole life.

A small mantel clock with a glass face, and a picture of a flower on the glass, ticked sedately on the shelf above this silent woman's bed. The above-mentioned houseguest at Hrísbrú could hear that ticking all his life afterward, whenever he had a moment's peace to listen inwardly; until he finally collapsed out on the road.

20

On Mound Robbery

When Finnbjörg died, Farmer Ólafur sent his son Andrés to meet with the parish priest of Lágafell Church, the church down the valley that had long since become the Mosfellsdalur residents' parish church by law. Ólafur said that he'd become too poor-sighted to make out the Lágafell priests clearly enough to grab them and give them a pounding. Andrés was also tasked with informing the priest that his father was determined to bury his wife in the Mosfell Church churchyard and it was up to the Lágafell priest whether he dragged himself there on the specified day and conducted the service; otherwise he, Ólafur of Hrísbrú, would do it himself. In brief, this business was not taken unamiably by the relevant authorities.

Now, when the body of the housewife has been laid in its coffin and carried to a storehouse and the farm is empty and everything is sorted and settled, said Stefán Þorláksson, and the day of the funeral approaches, Farmer Ólafur calls to his sons and foster son and poses them a task.

It was previously mentioned here in these pages that there had been a rather large quagmire in front of the walkway at Hrísbrú, and no one had measured its depth, nor were the boundaries clear between it and a sizable dung heap and gutter that was overflowing with semiliquid manure and had been doing so for a long time. The manure gutter had never been fully emptied as far as anyone remembers. Now it so happens that Farmer Ólafur sends his team there with the necessary tools and instructions to start digging and scooping, saying that they mustn't stop until they come to a treasure hidden deep within it.

They go and start digging into that muck, and it's pointless to describe such work here, what with the passage of years and no one in Iceland knowing any longer what a manure gutter is. Wouldn't the same apply to dirty jobs as was written earlier about difficult tasks? In the past, no jobs were called messy except those done unconscientiously by a careless worker and that bore the stamp of a good-for-nothing and slouch. Now, whether the men scooped and dug for a long time or not will not be dilated on here—what mattered is that finally, they got so far down into that awful morass that their spades hit something hard, with a clang. They reach down, grab the object and pull it from the mire, then go and place it on the wall nearest the door. They stand there pondering this object until finally deciding to go ask Farmer Ólafur his opinion. He turns the object over in his fingers regardfully for a while, until realizing that it's a church bell. He says that this bell must be cleaned carefully and then polished. Then he went into the family room and took the bell's clapper from the bottom of the housewife's chest.

Stefán Þorláksson has told about the morning when he accompanied his foster-father Ólafur to Mosfell to make the necessary preparations before the funeral procession arrived. It was around summer solstice. Old Red was brought in from the pasture and was standing there rather big-bellied in the farmyard. A saddle was placed on him outside the open storehouse, from which all sorts of junk had been cleared to make room for the coffin. Ólafur's sons led their father out of the farmhouse, while he himself carried the bell in his arms; it quickly regained the verdigris associated with true Christianity.

Ólafur's sons held their father's stirrup and helped him onto Red's back. Then they placed the bell in his arms, while making sure that he could still grip the horse's mane. The household's foster son was then told to lead the old man up the road to Mosfell and stop there on the hill outside the lychgate to the Mosfell churchyard. The district's residents had barely risen from bed and the golden plover, the bird of spring, ran alongside them over the Scree and whistled softly, but the bell's clapper was loose and clanged shrilly when Red stumbled over a rock on the road. Farmer Ólafur didn't stop at the Mosfell farmhouse, but had his foster son lead him to the lychgate, still carrying the bell in his arms. He said that Red should be tied to a fencepost to keep him from wandering onto the homefield, "…because now that my priests are no longer here, I never graze my animals on the Mosfell fields," he said.

They tied the bell tightly with string to the lychgate's crossbeam. But since the bell was missing its yoke, which any bell must have so that it swings freely and rings out in sustained notes when its rope is pulled, Ólafur finally had to remove the clapper and tap the bell's exterior with it. But even though the sound was muted and a bit dull, it was still the ringing of a bell, and the sound of Mosfell Church. As the cortege approached, Ólafur began ringing the bell. He kept on ringing it as the casket was carried in through the lychgate. He rang it as the people trickled into the churchyard. He rang it as the casket was lowered into the ground, as the priest cast earth over it, and as the people trickled away from the grave, while distractedly holding out his free hand to those who greeted him and extended him their sympathies, until his foster son, who was sitting on a tussock, told him that now the last person had gone and it was all over. Thus did Farmer Ólafur of Hrísbrú ring the entire community into the Mosfell churchyard and back out of it.

A week later, Ólafur made the same trip, this time in a shroud, to meet his wife. His son Bogi now carried the bell in his arms before his father's casket, fastened it to the lychgate's crossbeam as his father had done the week before and rang it as his father had rung it until it was over, then untied the bell from the crossbeam and carried it back home to Hrísbrú.

21

Of Gold and Hot Water

The road isn't always as smooth as the first knife trades of youth; the sticklebacks in Ash-Láki's barrel still wouldn't turn into sharks. Although Stefi wasn't lacking in transactions, and although he eventually acquired a speedier car than the one that took three days to get to Þingvellir, he was in fact stuck in a rut. Who could afford to take a taxi in those days? At least not respectable people of the sort who demonstrably had the money for lifts. Perhaps mainly the gang of grands seigneurs with license from society that drunken sots in Iceland have long constituted, and who had to go out into the countryside to drink dog medicine from the bottle on a tussock in the middle of a heath, kicked out by their wives; or else a few whippersnappers who all chipped in for a drive up to the Skólavarða tower and south to Skerjafjörður, and young girls who thought their good looks earned them a free ride. Hrísbrú continued to be Stefi's refuge, even though he'd become one of the country's very few motorists and pioneers of a new age. Countless were the days when he lay yet again on his back under a car, or stood hunched over one with his nose in its engine, and then got to sleep at home at night, while other farmers' sons had left the nest to become laborers in the south and saw money every day.

Until an event occurred in the capital that few people had expected, when Ash-Láki kicked the bucket and stopped carrying ashes and collecting rainwater in a barrel.

When it came time to dispose of the transport man's possessions following his funeral, Stefán Þorláksson was called upon to act as executor, along with the authorities. The deceased had just one suit, his Sunday best, thought to be forty years old but like new. Apart from that, there were his canvas work clothes, highly worn and darned with sailmakers' stitches, but which did not appear to have been specked or stained in any way in all those years. There were numerous boxes of rusty nails that the deceased had found on the road or pulled out of rotten planks and worked on straightening during his sparse leisure time, as well as on high holidays. He also left behind a considerable quantity of old bread at various stages of aging, from relatively freshly moldy bread, covered in green or gray detritus that would nowadays be classified as penicillin, all the way back to bread from the previous century that had long since begun to petrify. There was also the water barrel mentioned earlier. The man's wheelbarrow, invented by the Chaldeans in continuation of astrology, wasn't counted.

For a long time, the executors overlooked old crates stacked behind the vestibule door, some made of wooden slats, others of cardboard, most marked Thomsens Magasín, the name of a Danish store that had been here in the previous century. Some of the officials said that it would just be a waste of time opening anything more in this place. Yet, just for good measure, it was decided to try a few of the boxes from Thomsens Magasín. It turned out that those boxes were full to bursting with pressed silver, one box on top of the other.

Most of it was 25-aurar coins, but there were also huge amounts of 50-aurar coins, one-króna coins, two-krónur coins, even ten-krónur gold coins in among them, each coin carefully wrapped in a little piece of newspaper. Now was not the time to go home to eat and sleep; more officials had to be fetched to count the money. Finally, the money was taken to the city magistrate's office, following the substantial task, taking many people several days, of stacking the coins by size and wrapping them into rolls. This silver turned out to be worth 40 thousand gold krónur. Ash-Láki's gold propelled Stefi to a prominent position in both his foster-district and the entire nation and provided firm footing for his enterprising spirit, his high-mindedness and generosity, which became nationally known. As stated earlier, there is no way to tell the story of Stefán Þorláksson in a few pages about lost trifles in Mosfellsdalur. For that, another person must undertake to write a bigger and better book.

With his inheritance, Stefán Þorláksson built an auto garage for the capital south of Grímsstaðaholt. It had some of the thickest cement walls in Iceland and a floor area larger than any other building in the country up to that time. In this garage, car owners could keep their vehicles sheltered from the weather and wind all year round, and have constant access to them, dry and clean, if they wanted to go for a pleasure drive, for example on the First Day of Summer or Merchants' Day. They could also go there and stroke their cars and polish them, clean their joints and grooves with a toothpick when they had the time, or simply stand there and look at them; they could also lie down beneath them and repair them if they so desired. With better care for cars, the number of them in the capital increased rapidly in those years.

At that time, the city of Reykjavík had set up a model farm for potato cultivation in Mosfellsdalur, but no potatoes grew. The business went belly-up, as can be read in the papers from those days. For a long time, the farm's failure was mentioned in the same breath as the great peat extraction at Kjalarnes as proof of how everything in public sector goes bankrupt apart from the tax office.

Then it came to light that the capital's model farm had been built on the most unpropitious patch of land in the Mosfell district, Hlaðgerðarkot, where the sun doesn't shine. Originally, unruly bulls that belonged to the priest were kept in a stone paddock there, and it was never intended that people occupy the place. But it did have a warm stream; and in the sand where that stream flowed into the river, the priest's madam's bread was baked for several centuries, as was mentioned earlier in these pages. After some time had passed, turf huts were erected on that site for the needy people of the Mosfell district, and a story was made up about a woman who had settled there in the ancient past, Madam Hlaðgerður. There had never been anything but wretches at Hlaðgerðarkot, but never any quite so utterly piteous until the nation's capital put itself into millions in debt in its attempt to cultivate potatoes there. Stefán Þorláksson saved the nation's capital and the public sector from this miserable model farm by letting the city have his garages on Grímsstaðaholt, which always stood empty, in exchange for Hlaðgerðarkot, along with the stately country house that the capital, in a moment of distraction, had built for orphans there on a grassy patch by the river.

The capital hadn't noticed until too late that not only could bread be baked in the sand there for priest's wives, but that Hlaðgerðarkot was located in one of the world's most active geothermal areas; belonging to that miserable little croft were hot springs with a sufficient volume of water to heat New York City. Geothermal energy is different from a coal mine in that the mine is destroyed as more coal is extracted until it finally goes bankrupt, whereas the volume of water in boiling hot springs doesn't change for millions of years, regardless of how much or how little water is drawn from them. It is now known that the entire capital can be heated with boiling water that gushes up in torrents, free of charge, from the earth there year after year. The city is now turning to Stefán again with an offer, this time to purchase spring water from him to heat the capital and thereby eliminate the use of coal and oil in Iceland. For that water, Stefán was paid a greater sum of money than anyone had ever heard of in this country. The water was pumped south through large pipes, with the result that such an enormous quantity of boiling-hot bathwater is delivered to every individual in the city of Reykjavík that nothing else like it is known on earth except in Petropavlovsk in Kamchatka. For example, in a small house such as the one where this chronicle is being written, 17,280 liters of boiling water from Stefán Þorláksson's hot spring flow in and out every twenty-four hours.

22

Mosfell Church Redescends

When Stefán Þorláksson became the administrator of the Mosfell district and settled into his hot-spring farm in the valley, he towered so high over everyone else in the community that no one had done better since Egill Skallagrímsson buried his good chests there in a muddy quagmire; history calls them chests of silver out of a kind of timidity, but I'm quite sure they were chests of gold. On his farm, Stefi cultivated tomatoes, roses, and cows, and he collected all the machines that he was able to track down before anyone else did, and that many people would say made life both easy and shoddy. What those machines shared in common was that all you had to do was a press a button and they would do everything themselves; horsepower by the thousands. Refrigerators were found not only in the living room, kitchen, and bar, but also in the bedroom. What's more, a hall full of cars led off from the bedroom. Standing in the farmyard were trucks with numerous wheels, mountain vehicles and other tracked apparati, tractors, excavators, bulldozers, snowplows, and so on. Stefán owned a large herd of horses and enjoyed giving people horses as a sign of friendship. So capable a district administrator he was that you'd have to spend a long time paging through the *Biographies of District Administrators* to find another one like him. If he heard that a farmer was snowed in, he was there with his snow plow. If a farmer was so drunk all winter that he forgot to fertilize his homefield, Stefán would bring him money in late April to use to buy manure. Stefán never wanted to marry any of his housekeepers, in fact, but on the other hand, would sometimes give them a home and sometimes a husband when they left his employ. He gave sewing machines to good housewives and horses to pretty girls. There was hardly a woman in the community, young or old and no matter how inconspicuous, that he would not bring a double bouquet of roses on her birthday. Consequently, he was made an honorary member of the Women's Club. Now and again he would buy small, poor mountain farms that had long been deserted, turn them into estates and then sell them at a loss, or else give them to unrelated folk, sometimes with enough livestock for the new owners to live abundantly until they went bankrupt. At his disposal he had sheds full of all sorts of goods, like a well-stocked wholesale store, if needed for himself or others. "Buy, buy, no matter the cost" was his motto.

Sometimes his purchases were a mystery to people, not least when he bought a number of copies of something that most everyone else thought was of little value. Inevitably, even the most uninteresting things ended up multiplying in value in his possession—often, therefore, proving the theory of some economists that everything has been rising in price since the days of the Roman Empire. As an example of this, it may be mentioned that he undertook to build a library, despite never having been much for books.

It was at that time that Reverend Jón Þorgeirsson's great work, *Biographies of Remarkable Horses in Húnavatn County*, was printed at Vatnsdalshólar. Unfortunately, not a single copy of this book was sold in this country when it was published, and it remained that way for many years. Stefán Þorláksson read the book and liked it very much, being the horseman that he was. To show his love for literature, he bought three hundred copies of this book and placed them on the shelves of a library that he had fitted up for that purpose. This news traveled widely and sparked people's interest in owning the book, but as it turned out, the majority of the copies printed had been destroyed in a fire, and Stefán had bought the rest; in other words, there was now a serious shortage of the book in the country. Eventually, the book cost about as much as the Skrauthólar edition of the New Testament, and in the end, this library of Stefán's was sold for a huge sum after his death.

The same went for Stefán's purchase of Black Death. It was in the early days of the state monopoly on spirits in Iceland. Back then, humor wasn't entirely dead in this country, and the state monopoly that was then established to sell spirits, and which was run by the Good Templars, came up with the clever idea of putting onto the market a liquid that they first called the Great Plague, but that later went by the name Black Death. It was considered a top-notch schnapps. This liquid's name was printed in white letters on a pitch-black label, and below the name were two crossed femurs plus a skull, also printed in white. This was in fact the last grand-scale joke that Icelanders came up with, or, as one good man said, you could laugh at it with your whole mouth. But the numbness in the nation's brain, which is the curse of modern times, had begun to fester and it wasn't long before this product label was changed by the shy, soulless office workers from the countryside who had then begun to infiltrate the hierarchy. They had the Black Death label with the skull removed and put a sapless color image of a flower from the textbook *Botany* on the schnapps bottle, because they thought it would sell better that way.

Stefán Þorláksson was always the first person to grasp a joke. During the short time that Black Death with a skull and femurs was on the schnapps bottle, he seized the opportunity and built up a rather impressive cellarful of this drink for his own amusement and even to offer to his friends on festive occasions, although he himself never actually drank schnapps. Within a short time, Icelandic Black Death with the black label became famous the world over and still is; in many countries, this Icelandic product is the only thing anyone knows or wants to know about Iceland. Nowadays, Americans will pay 100 dollars for one such label from an old Icelandic schnapps bottle. Somehow, Stefán had realized early on what an excellent investment opportunity it was. Not only has that label, so ingeniously conceived, become more valuable than any other label of the same size in Iceland, but the nominal value of the schnapps itself has increased from 6.75 krónur, which was how much a bottle cost when Stefán bought his stock of it, to just over 400 krónur now. In the end, Stefán's Black Death turned out to be even more substantial of a windfall than the *Biographies of Remarkable Horses* by Reverend Jón of Vatnsdalshólar and even the love stories of Guðrún Trekkvindsdóttir, which will not be gone into further here; this came to light on the day that Stefán Þorláksson's estate was settled. Stefán's motto, "Buy, buy, no matter the cost" held up as usual, as did the theory that everything has been increasing in price since the days of Caligula.

These examples of foresightful financial speculation are not cited here to prove or disprove Stefán Þorláksson's excellence; we'll leave that be. But when his will was read after his death, both Black Death and Reverend Jón's horse book were definitively listed among the items that made up his possessions.

At this point in the story, I cannot refrain from repeating what was said earlier, that no one in the district was aware of

Stefán Þorláksson ever having spoken a word from the Bible in his life; a certain priest told the undersigned that this Stefán was as irreligious as Constantine the Great, who, however, demonstrably saved Christianity. At least for now it would be considered excessive to count him among the heroes of the faith in the Mosfell district. Yet he became a stronger pillar of true Christianity in this district, measured in krónur and aurar, than most of our holy men did either through silent prayer, exuberant hymn singing, or long sermons. In fact, Stefán Þorláksson stipulated in his will that the rather large amount of assets he left behind should be used to build a large and good church at Mosfell in Mosfellsdalur, there on the ruins of the old churches that keep the head of Egill Skallagrímsson.

23

Epilogue

On April 4, 1965, at the consecration of the new Mosfell Church, a bequest of Stefán Þorláksson and one of the most beautiful and best-equipped churches currently standing in Iceland, it received various splendid gifts. Most of these gifts came from families in the parish, the descendants of those who had once seen their church, in which they had put their faith, leveled to the ground here on its hill. Now a new generation celebrated the church of its ancestors, which had been rebuilt on that same hill, or, better put, had descended from that high field where it had towered over Mosfellsdalur for a time, looked after by three ruminating lambs.

Among these gifts were many treasures, some of precious metal, some artistic works of genius, including chandeliers and candlesticks, flower vases and paintings, as well as vestments and cloths; an outstanding baptismal font made of silver, on a pedestal.

The church itself is paneled from floor to ceiling with expensive, beautifully worked wood, and the pews are all softly padded. Heating pipes are hidden in the walls and floor. Bells without clappers ring if you press a button, either immediately, or they can be set in advance for a specific time, what with a clock being built into the mechanism.

Now the button has been pressed. The sun gleams on the colorful tops of cars parked in a dense cluster around the house of God and out in the farmyard and homefield. But it also shines through the window of Mosfell Church as in the old days, when there were no cars and no one knew what the word "difficult" meant. Since, according to the almanac, it is a summer month, and although the summer months are mainly about sheep, the golden plover, the bird of spring, which ran alongside Ólafur of Hrísbrú as he rode with the bell in his arms over the Scree, still dares to chirp in a timid but hopeful voice from Kirkjugil Ravine.

It must not be neglected to state that the above-mentioned old bell came home to stay yesterday. Old Ingimundur of Hrísbrú, one of the sons-in-law of those former Hrísbrú men, returned it the evening before the consecration in the same self-evident manner as one would deliver the priest his lamb on May 10.[14]

It is a crown bell, so-called by some because the canons by which the bell is connected to the yoke rise from the bell's head in stout copper loops, forming a six-spoked crown. The bell in question here is beautiful of form, but is coarsely made and has a rough texture. Neither clapper nor crown is cast, but only carelessly hammered; two decorative bands running around the waist, above and below, are crooked, for the most part, made in the mold freehand, by eye. It has been a long time since such primitive working methods in copper casting were employed in countries from which Icelanders have received church bells. It would be interesting to know where such bells have been cast since around the year 1000. Perhaps the bell is so old that this wasn't the first time it had lain in a dung heap for several generations; and therefore, not the first time either that another world and other saints and another religion had come into the picture when it was hung up again. The bell was hung in the choir, to the left of the altar, in this new church. There is no doubt that this bell reverberates with a sound from ancient times. The priest said that he was personally going to ring it at christenings because its voice was so beautiful as it faded. It is a small bell: external height, 34 cm; diameter 24 cm. Its tone is ample, long and clear, quivering as it dwindles.

A silver chalice stands on the altar. It is a well-crafted chalice, height 18½ cm, cup diameter 11½; foot diameter 13 cm. In the middle of the stem, a thick band encircles the joint where the cup is screwed to it, and soldered to this band is a ring with notches all around it. Such notches made for decorative purposes are sometimes called friezes and consist of a series of vertical lines.

The undersigned asked the priest who it was that had donated this chalice, but he didn't recall clearly who brought it, although he did remember that a certain elderly farmer from here in the district had found this object amid the rubbish left by an old woman who was dependent on the district and died in 1936, when she was in her eighties. No one had known that this destitute old woman had any valuables in her possession until her death, much less how this chalice had come into her hands, and least of all for whom she was keeping it. In fact, this was the woman who had once asked: "Can one ever be faithful to anyone but oneself?" Thirty-five years ago, some old men said that they recognized the object, and that it was the old chalice from Mosfell Church. So ends this miracle book.

Summer 1970; drafted in Rome 1963

Endnotes

1 The word "Tjaldanes" can be translated as "tenting point" (where people put up tents). Egill Skallagrímsson is a famous Viking Age farmer and poet, and the eponymous hero of the medieval Icelandic *Saga of Egill Skallagrímsson*, written between 1220-1240 and relating events that occurred between 850-1000.

2 Iðavöllur: in Old Norse mythology, the name of a meeting place of the gods. The poem *Völuspá* (*Seeress's Prophecy*) in the medieval collection of Old Norse mythological and legendary poetry, the *Poetic Edda*, says that the gods will meet on Iðavöllur again after the doomsday battle of Ragnarök, and there build a new city, Gimlé.

3 Bæsá: the spelling in this book of the farm and churchstead Bægisá, in northern Iceland.

4 The Icelandic word "fimm" means five. One meaning of the word "björg" is as the plural of "bjarg," which means a rock, crag, boulder, or cliff.

5 Gunnar of Hlíðarendi: a famous hero from the medieval Icelandic saga *Njáll's Saga*.

6 Washed-knickers water: an Icelandic term for weak coffee (i.e. "graywater," wastewater from baths, the laundry).

7 Gróa of Leiti is a character in Jón Thoroddsen's (1818-1868) novel *Piltur og stúlka* (*Boy and Girl*) published in 1850 and considered the first modern Icelandic novel. Gróa is a tremendous gossip, and later, gossips all over the country were given this moniker.

8 Gyra et reversa...: From *De Imitatione Christi* (*The Imitation of Christ*) by Thomas à Kempis (ca. 1380-1471), Book III, Chapter 13 (translated variously as "...spin me forward and spin me back," "...turn me about whichever way You will," "Lead me and turn me withersoever thou wilt," etc.).

9 Mossvell: This spelling of "Mosfell" reflects Guðrún's pronunciation of the word.

10 Moskó: A nickname for Mosfellsdalur, which Laxness mentions in his memoir *Í túninu heima* (*In the Fields of Home*) as stemming from a "misguided disdain for Russia."

11 Mókolla: a name for a ewe (or cow), russet-colored and hornless.

12 Vassmýri: the spelling in this book of Vatnsmýri, an area in Reykjavík (now the name of a nature reserve near the University of Iceland).

13 Fróðá Marvels: A series of supernatural events that took place at the farm Fróðá on the Snæfellsnes peninsula. These events, including dead men rising from their graves and the sky raining blood, are told of in the medieval Icelandic saga *Eyrbyggja Saga*.

14 May 10: In the old days in Iceland, farmers were obligated to keep a lamb over the winter for the parish priest, and then deliver it to the priest on the day known as "eldaskildagi," which was on the 10th of May every year.

archipelago books

is a non-profit publisher devoted to
promoting cross-cultural exchange through innovative
classic and contemporary international literature
archipelagobooks.org

elsewhere editions

translates luminous picture books from around the world
elsewhereeditions.org